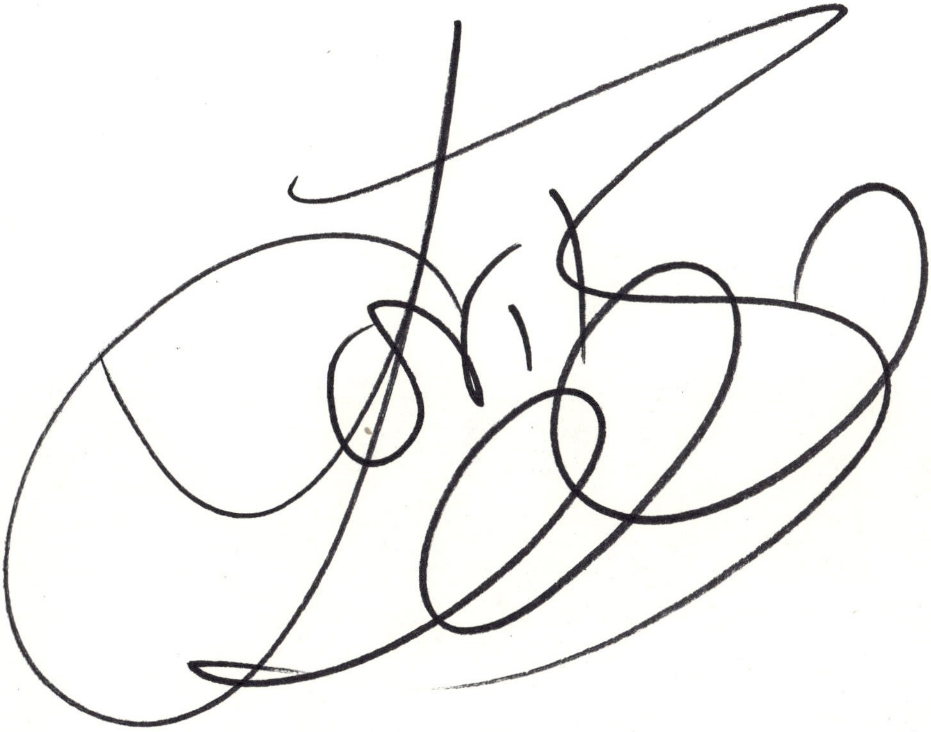

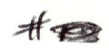

The One You're Waiting On

Lori Bell

This book is a work of fiction. Names, characters, places and incidents are the product of the author's imagination or are used fictitiously. Any resemblance to actual events, locales, or persons, living or dead, is coincidental.

Copyright © 2017 by Lori Bell

All rights reserved. This book or any portion thereof may not be reproduced or used in any manner whatsoever without the express written permission of the publisher except for the use of brief quotations in a book review.

Cover photograph by CanStockPhoto

https://www.nhlbi.nih.gov/health/health-topics/topics/pace/whoneeds
http://www.medtronic.com/us-en/patients/treatments-therapies/pacemakers/getting.html
https://www.kidney.org/atoz/content/nephrectomy
http://www.rightdiagnosis.com/p/postoperative_hemorrhage/basics.htm

Printed by CreateSpace

ISBN 978 1545029169

DEDICATION

To those of you who have found your gift and understand that your purpose is to give it away.

Chapter 1

Audi Pence closed the door to the only bedroom on the third floor of the Bed and Breakfast Inn. That entire floor was off limits to guests, and had been for as long as Audi could remember. The private area was her grandmother's living quarters. She stepped away from the closed door and walked on the barnwood flooring, barefoot with pale pink polished toes. A nurse, who wore navy blue scrubs with matching clogs on her feet, had followed her out into the hallway.

"So, my Gran... she's improving, right?" Audi already knew the answer to that. Her grandmother had suffered a heart attack. Running a B&B for nearly forty years had suddenly come to an abrupt halt. The seventy-eight-year-old woman was not accustomed to just sitting around, doing nothing. But, she was now looking at a minimum of eight weeks to do precisely that while she focused solely on her recovery.

"Somewhat, yes," the stocky nurse with short, spiked gray hair replied, as she stood in the dimly lit hallway, clenching her handbag on her arm. Her twelve-hour daytime shift ended at six o'clock every evening. "She's taking her medication without complaint, she's forced to eat healthy but curses like a sailor because of it, and exercise will gradually come when she's stronger." The nurse, whose name was Jo, had a full face and round cheeks with over applied rouge. Her eyes were kind. Her facial expression was almost always stoic. And Audi liked her. More importantly, she trusted her to care for her Grandma Besa. "If that's all, I really have to go."

"Oh, of course, yes. See you tomorrow." Audi watched the nurse rush the length of the hallway and descend the stairway.

Audi made her way down to the main floor. She stepped over a few plastic Barbie dolls, two were stark naked and one was wearing a formal gown with her hair a knotty mess. The piles of doll clothes and accessories momentarily annoyed her. But she quickly reminded herself that her six-year-old daughter had to have something to do while they spent time there. Living at the inn for the next couple of months was going to require some adjustment for both of them.

Audi turned the deadbolt on the front door and flipped the wall switch for the outside lights on the wraparound porch. She wasn't expecting guests as the inn had been closed for the past two weeks, ever since her grandmother fell ill. Even still, people drove by and stopped, looking for a place to stay, but the temporarily closed sign had turned them away.

The One You're Waiting On

Her grandmother's words rang in her ears once more. "Open this place up again. Run it for me, until I can get back on my feet and do it myself." It was a lot of work, but Audi was prepared to tackle it. That was part of the reason why she and her daughter had come there. She had spent the last week deep cleaning the entire second floor, all six bedrooms with adjoining bathrooms. She knew what was expected of her. *Provide guest accommodations for the night and a meal in the morning.* But that wasn't all.

Along with food service and housekeeping duties, Audi would have booking and customer service responsibilities. She was expected to provide guest check-in, check-out, and so many other amenities that Audi had made an endless list as she sat beside her grandmother's bed, listening to her recite it all. *Or maybe it was more like she barked the orders.* As she prepared for this, it became more obvious that her grandmother must have had her hands terribly full. Year after year. And she never once made it look anything less than easy. Audi was most nervous about managing the income, expenses and revenues. As a B&B owner, her grandmother never had permanent paid employees. She cooked, cleaned, and handled the business end of it all. *No wonder she had a heart attack.* Audi shook that thought from her mind. *Stop. It can't be that stressful.*

Tomorrow, when she turned that *CLOSED* sign around to *OPEN,* Audi would find out exactly what it was like.

"Mommy!" Audi followed the little voice calling from the kitchen.

"Berkley, what is all this?" Audi smiled and stared long at the little girl with blue eyes and curly platinum blonde hair, just like her own. The round kitchen table was set with two glasses of milk, and two paper plates with heaping amounts of macaroni and cheese on them. Audi had left the covered pot on the stovetop. And her daughter had served it. Audi wasn't planning to eat a bite of those starchy, fattening noodles, but when she saw the smile on Berkley's proud face, she sat down, grabbed her fork, and indulged.

"Do you like it, mommy?" Berkley asked, with too big of a forkful of noodles in her own mouth.

"It's delicious!" Audi replied, winking at her little girl who, in turn, giggled.

Berkley seemed happy there. She had brought along almost all of her toys from home. There also were two children her age, one girl and one boy, in the neighborhood that she was slowly getting to know through scheduled play dates. Berkley already made more friends in the Village of Maryville, Illinois than Audi. But Audi was a grown woman and not there to socialize. She and Berkley had a home in St. Louis, and the inn was just going to be a temporary arrangement for them. In eight weeks, her grandmother would be back on her feet and running the place again. Audi had no doubt.

~

The porch light was off. Her grandmother was asleep in her upstairs room, with a bell on the nightstand beside her bed in case she needed anything. The nights were usually quiet there, but Audi slept lightly regardless. Her room was tucked in a back, far corner on the main floor. There was a private hallway that led from the guests' sitting room, and the only area at the end of it was a space her grandmother had been using as an office. It was spacious, with a desk, book shelves, a reasonable-size closet, and a comfortable couch that folded out and into a bed. Audi was sharing that bed with her daughter. It was a way to keep her close in that big house, and to keep the rooms on the second floor undisturbed and ready for guests.

Berkley was sound asleep, arms and legs sprawled out and leaving very little room for Audi to lay there on her back, with her arms bent behind her head. She glanced at the baby monitor she had on the desktop. If her grandmother knew she had that device set up to keep a close watch on her, she would flip. Audi brought the monitor with her from home. She hadn't used it in years, not since Berkley was a baby. But, she needed it now, as she was committed to helping her grandmother make the strides to get well.

Audi remembered when she and Ben would lay close in the middle of their king size sleigh bed, their limbs entangled. She would take turns holding the video monitor with him, staring at the live black and white feed, and agreeing that they had the most beautiful baby girl in the world.

So much had changed in six years.

I need some time. That's what his note had said when Audi returned home the evening she found all of his belongings gone.

Chapter 2

Audi was startled from her sleep a few minutes before five a.m. The pipes in that eighty-something-year-old house always rattled when the plumbing was used. The current knocking sound, she knew, had come from a toilet being flushed upstairs. Her grandmother should not have been out of bed without assistance. Audi threw the covers back on her side of the couch-bed, glanced at her sleeping daughter, and raced out of the room, wearing only a Pink Floyd t-shirt and panties.

After taking double the steps at a time, she made her way up two flights of stairs to the third floor in just seconds. She flung open the door to her grandmother's room and found her sitting up in bed. Her snow white hair was wavy and thinning in spots, and it looked as if she had just run her hands through it to style it. Bed head had been her typical hairdo the past couple of weeks. She wore her bulky white terrycloth robe, completely underneath the covers, so Audi knew for certain she had been out of bed.

"Gran," Audi spoke, rubbing the sleep out of her own eyes, "you were up, weren't you?"

"Maybe," she replied with a smirk on her pale face. She looked considerably better today. *Stronger.* And she was sassy again.

"You could have fallen. You know I'm here for anything when your nurse isn't," Audi sat down in the pastel plaid armchair next to the bed. She attempted to tug at her short t-shirt, but gave up and crossed her legs on the chair instead.

"I'm feeling stronger and besides, you're not as light of a sleeper as you claim. I flush every morning before five a.m." Gran smiled. Her sass was gradually returning, and Audi was grateful. It meant her grandmother was getting well. Back to good health.

"Just be cautious, you could get lightheaded and fall – and you know a setback and this point would be foolish. This place needs you to run it." Audi felt nervous. Today was the day she would reopen Besa's B&B.

"Nurse Jo says some of the dizziness could be coming from being in bed all of the time. My body is used to moving," Gran attempted to explain.

"That could be partially true," Audi agreed, in an effort to appease her grandmother. But, she knew the heart attack had been the result of low blood pressure, and a low heart rate. She had been diagnosed with bradycardia because her heart rhythm was too slow and had caused insufficient blood flow to the brain. Her grandmother's reoccurring symptoms had been dizziness and lightheadedness before she had gone into cardiac arrest.

"I'd like to go downstairs today after my nurse gets here. I'll need her help making me look presentable first, of course."

Audi knew what her Gran was up to. She also was certain she was not yet capable of handling two flights of stairs. "Absolutely not. You just want to check up on me. No. If you want me to run this place, you have to allow me to flub up and learn as I go. I do not want you barking at me all day long." The relationship Audi and Gran shared was open and direct. Audi was more like her Gran than she cared to admit sometimes.

"So are you nervous?" Gran asked her.

"No," Audi lied. "We've been closed for fifteen days. We may not have a guest for awhile, until the word gets out that we are open for business again." Audi hoped that would not be the case. She had already made the extra effort to have a timely advertisement printed in the metro east newspaper, the Belleville News-Democrat, to announce the inn's reopening.

"Slow would be okay until you get the hang of things," Gran stated. "I am just two flights of stairs away though. Any questions, problems, or concerns…talk to me."

Audi was certain her grandmother would go crazy just sitting in bed when there was work to be done. But, she wanted to reassure her that she could handle it. Even if she wasn't yet completely convinced.

"I know, and I will need you," Audi replied, with a genuine smile. She realized how she needed to go easier on her Gran for wanting to be involved with the inn while she was recovering.

"Besides the reopening of this place wrecking your nerves, are you doing okay?" It was a sincere question, Audi knew, but she had spoken very little thus far about what weighed the heaviest on her mind. There just wasn't any good time to talk about it. *Her grandmother was sick, and asleep a lot. The nurse was in the room. Berkley needed attention.*

Audi ran her fingers through her blonde curls that were disheveled from sleeping. "I'm okay, yeah," Audi stated, once again tugging at the hem of her t-shirt as she twisted her body on the chair.

"Have you heard from the son of bitch?"

"Gran!"

"What? I was never a fan, you know," Gran admitted.

"I'm not sure I want to hear why not."

"The man is arrogant," she began. "He goes on like he

believes he's too good for people. And why? Because he can prance around in a business suit at the helm of a telephone company?"

"AT&T is more than just telephones, Gran," Audi smiled at how old school a woman of nearly eighty could be. The inn had WiFi, but only because Gran's best friend's grandson had come in and set it up after a customer had walked out when Gran didn't know *what the hell he was talking about*. She had not had a guest walk out in years.

"Have you heard from him since he left you and that beautiful little girl?"

"No," Audi inhaled a deep breath through her nostrils. She had called, left endless voice messages, and texts. Ben had not responded to any one of her pleas.

"Berkley told me her daddy's working," Gran stated, as a matter of fact.

"Yes, and that's all she will know for now. I can't even explain this to myself, so how I can I expect to help her understand?"

"Have you faced the fact that he's most likely getting horizontal with another woman?"

"Gran!" Of course the dreadful thought had crossed her mind too many times. But, it hurt to focus on. Or truly believe.

"That's always a man's reason to leave," Gran spoke gently.

"I have nothing to go on," Audi stated. "If he's with someone else, if he wants someone else, then he at least should have the balls to tell me. It's as if he's disappeared. I've called his work, and they only keep telling me that he's taken a leave of absence." Audi shook her head and twisted on the chair again. She gave up tugging on her short t-shirt and just let her panties show. Her legs and rear end were shapely and fit. Not that Gran cared either way.

"Do you still love him?"

"As much as the first time I realized I had fallen hard." Audi felt the tears pool in her eyes.

"Did you sense he was pulling away before he left? Was he still reaching underneath that short little t-shirt when you were beside him at night?"

"Gran, please," Audi said, feeling her cheeks flush. She never did talk about *that sort of thing* with her grandmother.

"Oh for chrissakes, I'm a woman, too, honey. And your grandfather was not the only man I allowed to ravish me." Audi lifted her eyebrows and let out a slight giggle. Just the thought of her heavy-set grandmother in the buff in bed with a man made her want to forcefully dismiss that image before it entirely entered her mind.

"Yes, we shared intimacy, you know, like married people do," Audi said, feeling uncomfortable discussing it. "Sometimes we're tired, busy with a child, and work. It came and went for us during our seven-year marriage, but it's common to have phases like that. It hadn't been that long since we…" Audi's words trailed off.

"Can I ask you something?" Gran inquired.

"May as well," Audi replied, still uncomfortable. Or annoyed. She wasn't sure which.

"I am your grandmother, yes, but think of me for a moment as just a woman." That was difficult for Audi to do. There, in that bed, sat a large woman with broad shoulders, and thick limbs. Her voice was deep. It was hard to imagine a feminine bone in her body. "Did you feel as if you, or Ben, were just going through the motions? After time, in many relationships, it happens. Your body wants the intimacy, but you can no longer connect your mind and your soul to someone. You touch, but you don't really feel." Audi sat there in complete awe. *Who was this woman sometimes?* "I know, because it happened in my marriage."

"You and Gramps were married for fifty-one years, until the day he died." As if she needed to be reminded. It had been eight years since Grandpa Art passed away. Audi's words implied immaturity, as if just because they had never separated or divorced, that meant they were blissful. Her grandparents, she recalled, at least appeared as happy together as two old people could be. Audi, just one year shy of thirty years old, still thought of mature adults as too ancient to enjoy that part of life. And she was about to realize how wrong she was.

"Yes, we were," Gran stated, "but that doesn't mean I was in love with him. I fell out of love during my marriage. We existed together. We made each other happy in endless ways. He believed I just no longer cared about sex. He lived with that."

"And what did you do?" Audi caught herself being as direct with her Gran as if they were discussing any other topic – aside from the always unmentionable. *Sex*.

"I had an affair for eleven years," she admitted her indiscretion without a shred of shame.

"Oh my God…" Audi's eyes widened and she sat up straighter on the chair, uncrossed her legs, and planted her bare feet firmly on the floor.

"We had a ground's man here," Gran attempted to explain, "He was from Glen Carbon," which was an adjacent city to Maryville, less than four miles away. "We were intensely attracted to each other. I've never known that kind of fire." Audi expected to feel embarrassed hearing that, but as she began to feel less flabbergasted, she was intrigued. There was much more to her Gran than she believed. "Just weeks after we hired him, I was sleeping with him. Stolen moments in this house, on the grounds. Jesus, honey, I could write a book."

Audi giggled, but she didn't mean to. She still felt such shock. "Gran, this is unbelievable. Did anyone else know?"

"No. We were discreet. It was our time to shut out the world. And then go back to our separate lives."

"That seems sad to me," Audi told her.

"No, it really wasn't. I never pined away for a man I knew I couldn't publicly be with. Not without hurting too many people. I had your grandpa to take care of. And my lover had his cherished ones. We just found something in each other that we couldn't deny. We relished it, but we never sacrificed for it. Does that make sense?"

"Yes and no," Audi admitted. "What are you trying to tell me? Do you think my husband sacrificed our marriage and family for someone else who gives him some sort of amazing feeling that I could not?"

"Yes and no," her Gran replied, and Audi tried to sense if she was being snarky.

"Your nurse is going to be here soon. I have to get ready," Audi stated, standing on the barnwood floor that creaked in front of her chair, near the bed where her grandmother remained tucked into. She didn't want to deal with this now.

"This conversation isn't over," Gran stated, forcing her granddaughter's eyes back to her.

"I'm not ready to face that. I don't even know what the truth is," Audi admitted, denying the tears that wanted to freefall from her eyes.

"When you are ready, I'm here."

Audi nodded her head. She wanted to say *thank you,* but the words didn't come.

"Remember something," Gran offered. "*Any which way you can* is not the woman you are."

"What do you mean?" Audi asked.

"Don't be a woman who holds on and lets a man love you any which way he can. Don't beg and plead for his attention and affection any which way you can. You're better than that. You deserve far more than that absentee husband of yours."

Audi wanted to tell her that she was full of surprises. *She was something else.* The advice her grandmother had just given her was astounding. And profound. Audi had so much to think about now. She walked over to the bed and hugged her grandmother tightly. And not another word was spoken.

Chapter 3

Audi's blonde hair was pulled up in a loose bun on top of her head, and she wore a plain white v-neck t-shirt with faded flared jeans, and brown flip flops on her feet. She walked back and forth on the wraparound front porch, holding a broom in front of her with both hands as she swept off the concrete for the tenth time. It was noon and there were no guests at the inn yet. She reminded herself that it was typical for overnight visitors to arrive in the evening. After all, a Bed and Breakfast was just a place to sleep and grab a bite to eat before leaving again.

The One You're Waiting On

The antique white siding on the B&B was spotless. The hunter green shutters looked as if they had just been brushed with a fresh coat of paint. The flowers in the landscape were in full bloom. The swingset, far out into the well-manicured yard, caught her eye as Berkley gave her a quick wave when she momentarily let go of the chain attached to the swing that was taking her high into the air. It was the same old swingset Audi remembered playing on as a child. The poles were not anchored into the ground and easily shifted the whole swingset unevenly off the ground if anyone were to pump their legs too high on those swings. As she saw this again just now, Audi called out a reminder for Berkley to – *be careful, don't swing so high.*

That sight took her back to when she and her mother would visit the inn. Gramps was an over-the-road truck driver and rarely at home if it wasn't the weekend. Gran always managed the inn alone. Audi wondered now if she had ever seen the groundskeeper. And exactly when did that eleven-year time frame of their affair take place? That story was still dominating her thoughts. *Gran had an affair. More than a decade of hot, forbidden sex with a man who was not her husband.* She was far from judging her Gran. After all, it was her life. If anything, Audi admired her for owning it. And, finally, she felt it was time for her to own hers as well.

Audi swept the concrete harder, bending the broom's uneven straw-like bristles a little too forcefully. She was beginning to feel less pity for herself. It had been seventeen days since her husband *needed some time.* The concrete on the porch at her feet was on the receiving end of her building anger, as Audi told herself she was no longer going to give in to her vulnerability to reach out to her MIA husband. *If he didn't want her and Berkley, to hell with him. He was the coward for running, for ignoring her, for abandoning his daughter, and for refusing to offer any explanation. She would continue to focus on raising her little girl, caring for Gran, and finally begin thinking of herself again.* She was beginning to feel stronger, like she could handle what was going on in her life. Audi definitely came to terms with one thing for certain – at the end of their couple-of-months-stay at the inn, she and Berkley were going home. With or without Ben.

~

Wes Delahunt had driven Interstate 70 from Cove Fort, Utah to St. Louis, Missouri at least a half a dozen times in the year and a half since he began writing a novel, set in St. Louis. This time, he had just gotten off the phone with his publisher and he was flustered as he drove. It had been too late to change lanes, traffic was congested, so instead of staying on Interstate 70, Wes had already merged with traffic on 270. *Dammit!*

Wes inhaled a deep breath, and kept both hands on the steering wheel, and his eyes on the roadside signs. *After almost nineteen hours on the road, it really didn't matter if he drove into St. Louis a little later than planned.* All he had waiting for him was a hotel room. His laptop was on the backseat. His suitcase was in the trunk. He traveled light each time he made this trip to the Gateway City. What he did there was take in his surroundings, walking or driving, and then he would retreat to his hotel room to write. He had promised his publisher, who was pressing him to meet a deadline, that this trip would be his last. He just needed a little more inspiration to finish his novel. *Okay, a lot more.*

The One You're Waiting On

Wes slowed his vehicle for a car in front of him that switched lanes. And then he glanced over at a billboard alongside of the interstate. The image of the Victorian-style house depicted on it looked breathtaking. *Historic.* It struck him. He had not ever seen that billboard. Well, he had not veered off course on this trip before.

2 miles ahead. Exit 12. Besa's Bed & Breakfast.

He passed by before he could read more. He was certain there had been a slogan, words strung together to coax travelers to venture off the interstate and stay the night at the B&B. Wes wasn't entirely certain that's what he would do, but he had less than two miles to talk himself out of taking the next exit and doing a drive by of that place. That picture-perfect place somehow struck him as inspiring. *Yes, inspiring! That's exactly what he needed right now. He hadn't felt like this. Like writing anything substantial. In a very long time.*

~

Audi held her cell phone to her ear as she walked through the kitchen. She just finished pouring a generous amount of canned tomato juice into a simmering crockpot of homestyle goulash. *It was important to have food prepared, warm and ready when you're open for business*, Gran had told her. On the opposite end of her cell phone, Audi was talking to her neighbor, back in St. Louis.

Phoebe Hunter was six years older than her with a husband and two teenage children. The Hunters were established in their house, located in the Tower Grove South St. Louis neighborhood, when Ben and Audi moved in. Audi remembered being eight and a half months pregnant, standing curbside in the front yard of her two-story colonial-style home, and having found an instant connection with Phoebe. That bond had only strengthened through the years of calling on each other. In fact, Phoebe was the first person Audi confided in when Ben left her.

Phoebe questioned her why the seventeen miles currently separating them felt like a country away. "Ugh, I know. I miss you too, Phoebs," Audi sighed into the phone. The two of them were accustomed to talking to each other every day. Since Audi had packed up herself and her little girl and moved into her Gran's B&B, a twenty-minute drive away, Phoebe had given her space. She didn't want to, but Audi had asked for it.

"Say the word and I'll come visit. I could be your first overnight guest," Phoebe giggled, well aware that this was an important day, the reopening of the B&B. But no one had checked in yet.

Audi laughed into the phone. "We don't do well when we spend the night together. I'd have to go buy more wine…"

"Maybe that's what you need. Just get drunk and say to hell with your husband and these feelings that have forced you out of your house and into a predicament that's going to tie you up for months." Phoebe knew that Audi wasn't entirely on board with her running the B&B. It was a huge commitment to go into half assed. And Phoebe had warned her of that the last time they spoke on the phone more than a week ago.

"I know you think this was too much for me to take on, and you're probably right," Audi admitted, "but I'm doing it for Gran. She needs me. And I need an escape. It's only for a couple of months."

"And then you and Berk are coming home?" Phoebe cautiously asked.

"Yes, we are."

"That's wonderful to hear," Phoebe stated, trying to contain her excitement. "There's another reason why I called, aside from missing you like crazy." Audi imagined Phoebe, sitting outside underneath her wraparound front porch on her dark brown wicker chair with the yellow floral cushion. It was a view she had seen from the front windows of her house too many times to count. Her feet were bare and her legs were likely up and curled under her bottom. Her long dark hair was probably down, as she ran her fingers through it while she spoke into the phone. "I've seen Ben."

Hearing those words immediately put Audi into a tailspin. She brushed away an annoying curl that had fallen over her eye. She probably should have pulled out a chair from the kitchen table and sat down, but instead she paced in between the table and the counter. "You have? Where? What did he say?" *Why hadn't she mentioned that several minutes ago when she called?* Audi's questions were endless, and this was going to be the first time since Ben left that those questions wouldn't be left ignored and unanswered.

"I didn't talk to him," Phoebe revealed. "I've only seen him come and go, twice now, from the house."

"So he's back home? He's living there again?" Audi could feel her heart pumping at a rapid speed.

"No, I don't think so. He's been there an hour or less at a time, maybe just to pick up things, it looked like."

"Why didn't you go over there? Or call me?" Audi couldn't hide the disappointment in her voice.

"The first time I saw him there, I debated to do just that for the entire hour his car was parked across the street on your driveway. And the second time, I had just come home when he was leaving. I hadn't been gone very long, so I know his trip home was short. I looked at him from my car, but he never glanced my way from his. Audi, are you upset with me?"

"With you? No," Audi answered her. "It's really not your place to fight my battles."

"But I would have…if I had known what to say," Phoebe admitted.

"You could have just confronted him and asked him why the hell he left me and his daughter, and where he's living, and for how long he plans to ignore my messages?" Audi could have gone on all day long.

"Are you still reaching out to him?" Phoebe asked.

"I haven't in the past twenty-four hours. I'm trying not to. How long has it been since he was home, and why didn't you tell me as soon as you saw him?" *Okay, so maybe she was a little miffed at her.*

"It was last week," Phoebe reluctantly admitted.

"Why the wait? Is it because I said I needed space? Phoebs, the fact that you saw Ben cancels out the time I need to think."

"When you picked up the phone today, there was a difference in your voice. You sounded happier, no longer terribly sad or depressed. I honestly debated telling you at all," Phoebe stated as a matter of fact.

"I do feel stronger. I had a talk with Gran. I'm also ready for customers in this building, but it's driving me a little bat shit crazy knowing every day could be hurry up and wait…for no reason at all. No one could show, day in and day out. I guess I'm trying really hard to keep my mind on other things and occupy my time. But now, you tell me you've seen Ben. He came home. Knowing that shoves me right back to where I was. I don't care about anything else but getting my husband back."

"For fuck sake! I never should have told you!" Phoebe regretted it, for sure.

"No, I needed to know, really…" Audi replied. "I'm just being honest with you because you're the only confidant I have. I am only able to tell Gran so much because she's still recovering."

"Okay, good. Just talk to me. Anytime. When you said you needed space, that hurt. I can't leave you alone when you're suffering like this. Promise me you will talk to me, every fucking day."

Audi giggled into the phone. Phoebe cursed like a sailor when she was scared or angry…or drunk. "Only if you promise to tell me the next time there is activity at my house."

Phoebe hesitated. "Okay, but I will tell you when I'm in my car, en route to picking you up, because I know you will fly over here like a bat out of hell, and if you wrapped your car around a tree because of me, I would never be able to live with the guilt."

Audi was laughing again. "Sounds like a good plan." In the meantime, Audi knew for certain she would debate taking a drive back to St. Louis to see what was missing from her home. *What else had her husband come back for? What could he not live without? What was more important than her and their daughter?*

Chapter 4

Audi had just come from the third floor of the B&B. She checked on Berkley, who she found playing dominoes in the living area with both Gran and Nurse Jo. Audi previously apologized to the nurse when her little girl repeatedly visited that floor throughout the day. But, she wouldn't hear of it. Nurse Jo had many explanations for why a child's company had a way of healing an elderly person. *She's young and vibrant and always brings a smile and laughter. That's the best medicine for your grandmother right now.* Somehow Audi didn't entirely believe the nurse wanted Berkley hanging around, all for the sake of her patient's health. It seemed that Berkley's company was something Nurse Jo thoroughly enjoyed as well. Because when Gran napped throughout the day, Berkley and Nurse Jo continued to play games.

That thought brought a smile to her face as she descended the final flight of stairs, and when her flip-flopped feet reached the main floor, Audi looked up to find a man standing at the desk near the front door. She had not heard anyone enter. The bell on the door never chimed, or she missed it. *In any case, she quite possibly had her first customer!*

"Hi, I'm sorry, I hope you weren't waiting long?" Audi brushed away that same defiant curl from her eye, as she continued to walk toward the desk near the door that was meant to be the spot for check-ins. She noticed one piece of luggage at the man's feet and a laptop, sans a case, balancing on top of it. He wore faded jeans with a hole in one knee, and a charcoal gray t-shirt with the lettering, *Comfortably Numb,* across his chest. Audi forced her eyes away from his shirt, but she was smiling inside. *Pink Floyd was her pick for damn good music, too.*

"Not at all. I just drove up, and walked in. Do you have a vacancy?" he asked, and Audi was half-tempted to tell him how he was her first customer because they had been closed for weeks. *But he didn't need to know her recent life story. Especially not the fallout.* He did have kind eyes, and an infectious smile that displayed some perfectly straight, bright white teeth.

"We do," Audi said, pulling back the chair in front of her. She rehashed the steps in her mind that Gran insisted she follow. *Will you be staying with us for one night only? How will you be paying for that? All rooms have an adjoining full bathroom. The kitchen and living area are yours to frequent. Dinner is on the stove. A moderate selection of drinks are in the refrigerator. Breakfast will be served at eight a.m. Had she forgotten anything?*

There was a chair on the opposite side of the check-in desk, too, and her first customer also sat down. His legs were stiff from driving too long, and he immediately popped back up and out of the chair. "Sorry, I need to stretch my legs. I'll stand and check in. I've been in my car too long."

"Where are you from?" Audi inquired. That may have been another thing Gran had mentioned. *To make small talk, find out where our travelers' roots are.*

"Cove Fort, Utah. Almost twenty hours from here."

"Oh my. So what brings you to Maryville, Illinois?"

"I'm actually en route to St. Louis. I just saw the billboard and thought this place might be a nice change of scenery for me. Hotels are stuffy sometimes."

"Ah, yes, I agree. I'm from St. Louis. This is actually my Gran's place, um I mean my grandmother," Audi smiled.

"I like it here already," he told her. "Truly inspiring."

Audi wasn't quite sure what he meant, but she smiled again anyway. His sandy brown hair and green eyes caught her attention almost as much as his Pink Floyd t-shirt. "So, one night, if that's what you're here for, is ninety-five dollars."

He reached around to the back pocket of his jeans to retrieve his wallet. "Yes, um, depending on your room availability, I may lodge here for my whole trip. I was planning to spend three nights in the city." *Her first customer wanted to stay more than one night. Audi hid her excitement. Gran will be happy to have steady business again.*

"That's perfectly fine. We have room for you. Did you want to pay per day or for all three nights ahead?" This part made Audi feel nervous. Dealing with money, and other people's decisions on whether or not to spend it, could be touchy.

"I'll pay for all three," he told her, handing over his credit card. The name on the card read, Wes Delahunt. He watched her facial expression. It had not altered. *She didn't know who he was. He liked it that way. It was a nice change of pace from his travels to the bigger cities.*

After Audi checked him in, she retrieved the key to his room. His would be the first one on the right at the top of the stairs. *May as well fill up the rooms in consecutive order,* Gran had told her so. She stood up and noticed he was only a couple of inches taller than her five-seven frame. She had also spotted flip flops on his feet earlier. The thought made her giggle inside. Gran had harped about her wearing *decent shoes* in the B&B. When really, Audi would have preferred to pad around in her bare feet all day and night. And she mostly had, until they were open for business.

"First room on the right at the top of the stairs. The second floor houses all of our rooms. The third floor is off limits for private living quarters." Audi made a mental note to attach the chain at the top of the stairwell later with the friendly sign that alerted customers of the private area. She also would have to warn Berkley and Nurse Jo about that, so they would not stumble over it.

"I understand. And thank you," he said, taking the bronze key from her. At that moment she questioned whether she had remembered to lock all six of the doors on that floor.

"You're welcome, Mr. Delahunt. I hope you enjoy your stay here." They both reached out to share a business-like handshake.

"Please, call me Wes."

She didn't know why, but she felt herself blush a little. The warmth of his hand on hers. The sparkle of his green eyes. His unkept sandy brown hair. The slight stubble growing on his face and chin. "Okay. I'm Audi. Sorry, I forgot to share that tidbit of information with you." She giggled nervously as their hands parted.

"Audi...that's a beautiful name. Sort of sounds like a book character..."

"Why thank you, but I can't say I've heard that before." She laughed, as he picked up his lone suitcase and tucked his laptop underneath his arm.

~

"Okay Gran, that just felt weird," Audi said, plopping down on the pastel plaid armchair at her bedside.

"How so?" she asked, as the two of them were now alone. Nurse Jo and Berkley had just happily exited and went into the next room to play Barbies. Even with her typical stoic expression, Audi could tell Nurse Jo adored her daughter. As

Gran's health gradually began to improve, Audi wondered if Nurse Jo was being paid to monitor the patient or play with the child? The thought made her smile.

"Well, he's very nice. I got the basic information from him, but I felt as if I needed to find out more. You know, since he's staying under our roof and all?"

Gran chuckled. "You'll get used to not giving a shit after a few more file in." Audi shook her head in agreement and laughed. *Maybe so, but Wes Delahunt had peaked her interest for sure.*

~

The next time Audi made her way down the two flights of stairs, she had Berkley with her. They were walking into the kitchen as Berkley complained about having to try the goulash that was prepared for dinner. "But I don't wanna eat that. I like my noodles without meat and all that other stuff like peppers and onions."

Audi laughed as she ran her fingers through the blonde curls on the top of her little girl's head. "Well what do you like with your noodles then?"

"Cheese!"

Just as Berkley exclaimed her preference, they entered the kitchen to find Wes Delahunt already there. He was seated at the table with a plate of that dreaded goulash Berkley had just spoken of. And Audi also noticed he had a glass of red wine. *Good choice,* she thought to herself. She too believed pasta and wine went hand-in-hand.

"Oh, hi," Audi spoke first as Berkley attempted to hide behind her. She wasn't always shy, but having their first customer had thrown her into a slightly timid state. Audi understood. His presence had thrown her, too. Despite her conversation with Gran, she was still confused by it. "Berkley, this is Mr., um Wes. He's our guest in Gran's B&B."

"Our very first guest?" Berkley expressed, and Audi didn't respond. She only kept on going with their introduction.

"Wes, this is my daughter, Berkley."

"Nice to meet you, Berkley," Wes said, as he stood up from his chair and simultaneously placed the napkin from his lap, onto the table.

He never made an attempt to reach out. He could see she was curious, but timid. "This is really good," he said pointing at his food on the table. First, he looked at Berkley and then at her mother. He already was learning more about his hostess. She had a daughter. And he again, just like earlier, noticed the diamond ring on her finger. His left hand, however, was bare.

"Thank you," Audi replied. She wasn't the most wonderful cook, but she refrained from admitting it. *Even her husband used to humor her.* "So, what do you say? You'll try it?" Berkley nodded her head.

Several minutes later, Berkley had eaten a small plate of goulash and drank her entire cup of milk, leaving behind obvious evidence of it with the white mustache above her lip. The whole time she ate, she talked nonstop to Wes. *She warmed up quickly to strangers.* He learned of her house in St. Louis, her neighborhood friends in the Tower Grove subdivision, and he also knew the name of her brand new friends not too far down the street from the B&B.

"I should go upstairs now," Berkley said, looking at her mother. Audi was seated at the table with them. "What time is it, mommy?"

Audi smiled at her, having read her little girl's mind. "Nurse Jo has thirty more minutes before her shift is over. If she's not too busy with Gran, I'm sure she will play a game with you. Ask nicely though."

Berkley said a quick goodbye to Wes and left the room. He laughed as he took the last swallow of red wine in his glass.

"What?" Audi asked him, knowing he was laughing in reference to Berkley.

"She's a delight. I respect how she suddenly wanted to leave the room – apparently for better company or a more enjoyable offer upstairs – and she just came right out and implied it's been fun, but we'll see ya."

Audi laughed out loud. "Yep, that's my girl." They chuckled together before Audi spoke again. "I should explain, I guess. My grandmother owns and operates this inn. She had a heart attack a few weeks ago, and is recovering upstairs. Hence, the nurse who plays games with my daughter."

"I see," Wes spoke, fingering his empty wine glass. "I'm sorry to hear that. I hope she has a complete recovery."

"Thank you. Me too. She's getting there." Audi eyed his glass. "Can I get you some more wine?"

"Thank you, but I can get it," he stood up and walked over to the refrigerator. "Will you have some as well?"

"Oh, I, actually, yeah that sounds really good right now." Wes noticed she had not eaten anything while her daughter ate her dinner.

"Do you not like goulash?" he asked, reaching for a glass on the counter for her, the same place he had found one for himself earlier. He poured the wine in her glass, and then refilled his on the table.

"I'm saving it for the guests," she replied, as she received the glass of wine from him and said *thank you* before she took her first sip. Wes wanted to ask if there were more guests on his floor, the only floor there with vacancies, but he refrained. He hadn't seen or heard anyone else. "So, tell me, what brings you from Utah to St. Louis?" After just a few sips of alcohol, her head already felt light. And then she remembered she had not eaten since breakfast when she toasted one half of an English muffin and slathered it with low-fat margarine.

"Work," he answered, with a crooked grin. "I'm a writer."

"Really?" She was fascinated. "We just don't hear that too often here in the Midwest. What do you write?" Audi was halfway through her glass of wine, and Wes noticed. Her sips were generous, and she truly seemed to indulge. Her figure looked as if she didn't treat herself to much else. Her fitted flared jeans and white v-neck tee gave him a glimpse of the body underneath.

"Novels, actually. My latest is set in St. Louis, and I've been looking for the inspiration for awhile now to finish it. Hence, my trips back and forth." He used the same wording as she had earlier, and she smiled.

"That's amazing!" Audi was intrigued to know a published author. "So, you said, your latest? Does that mean you have written other books?"

"Yes, three others. I escaped from being a starving author about five years ago."

Audi laughed, and then added, "So if I Googled your name, I'd find a best-selling author?" For a moment, she wondered if he had been disappointed she didn't recognized him. She knew of some male authors. Stephen King. Nicholas Sparks. It depended upon the genre. Audi did enjoy reading romance novels.

"Best-selling? Not quite. But I do okay. And, yes, anyone can throw together a webpage. I'm online."

"Do you have a pen name?"

"Wes Delahunt it is. What you see is what you get. I never wanted to change my name. I, quite frankly, like my name. Maybe not quite as much as I like yours though…"

She laughed. "Pence, by the way," she said, and he looked a little confused. "Audi Pence."

"Ah, the lady has a last name, too." He smiled. She smiled. "So where's your other half?" he asked, when he pointed to the diamond on her ring finger. It was impossible to miss a rock that size.

And that was the million dollar question.

Wes noticed her immediate discomfort, and he wished he had not asked. He obviously overstepped. "I'm sorry, forget I asked. It's none of my business."

"We've been married for seven years," Audi began, ignoring his apology. "It hasn't all been blissful, but we were a family. We loved each other." The wine was definitely taking over as Audi continued to speak without barriers. "Just a few weeks ago, I came home one night following a dance recital of Berkley's that my husband said he was going to miss because he had to work. I tucked my daughter into bed, and found a note on the dresser in my bedroom. 'I need some time.' That's all he had to say. He packed up and left. And, weeks later, I still do not know where he is, or what he's doing…or who he's with." It was all out there now. And it actually had felt good to share what had happened to her life with a stranger.

"I don't even know what to say. That's awful. That's cowardly." Wes never took his eyes off of her. "You deserve some answers."

"Thank you. I think so as well," she agreed. "But, my husband is not offering any. I've begged, pleaded, wished and prayed. I'm in a state of limbo right now."

"I'm sure you are," Wes said to her. "And I'm sure that's tough as a mother. Your daughter seems to be doing well. She's happy, I mean."

"She doesn't know. She thinks her daddy is working. The timing of spending several weeks here has helped. We are out of our element. Makes it easier to cope."

"I could see that. But, what happens when you have to go back? Will you be hit like a ton of bricks with the reality of this? Or will you have worked out some sort of acceptance deal with yourself because you've learned to live without him, period, whether you are here or there?"

"That's a deep question, Delahunt," Audi said seriously, and then she smiled. She liked the way his name rolled off of her tongue.

"One to ponder. No need to answer it now," he told her.

"I'd like to think of what I'm going through in terms of a cliché. The truth will set me free."

"Maybe," he told her. "But, regardless, the truth sometimes hurts."

"Have you ever been in love?" Audi asked him outright.

"Me? Um, I've never been married," he stalled his answer.

"Have you ever had your heart broken?" she pressed further.

"If you count senior year of high school when the first girl I had ever been with cheated on me with my cousin?"

"Ouch," Audi replied. "Did you love her?"

"At the time I thought so. But, nah, not really. Not the kind of love that makes your heart hurt something fierce when you're away from someone. You can't eat. You can't sleep until she's in your arms again."

That was beautiful. Audi was drawn to his sensitivity. "Sounds to me like you've been in love..." she told him.

"I'm a writer, remember?" he smiled.

"What genre?" she asked, feeling braver than earlier.

"Mystery, romance...with a few twists. A little bit of everything in more than one genre, but they've labeled me romance."

"Oh my," she answered. If business didn't pick up at the inn, she may have to spend some time reading a new author. "I hope you find the inspiration you're looking for here... in St. Louis, I mean," she told him, as she stood up from her chair at the table. With her sudden movement, she was quickly reminded how the wine had gone directly from her empty stomach to her head.

She swayed a bit, and Wes abruptly stood up and grabbed her by the arm. His hand on her skin sent a current through her that she had never remembered feeling before. Her eyes moved to his.

"You okay?" he asked.

"Yes," she answered. She saw him looking at her lips. And maybe she was staring at his too. He smelled like soap or possibly cologne. It wasn't aftershave because there was still stubble on his face that had drawn her in again.

She could hear her own heart beating in her ears. She saw him, felt him, inch closer to her. She watched his lips part, he wet them with the tip of his tongue, and then he drew back.

Berkley and Nurse Jo were noisily pouncing down the stairway. It was quitting time. *Time to stop allowing this feeling, whatever this feeling was, that so suddenly had taken over her mind…and body.*

"Good night, Miss Audi," Nurse Jo spoke from the next room. Audi walked to the open doorway between the kitchen and the living area. Her face felt flushed. She blamed the wine, but she knew better.

"Have a good evening, Nurse Jo. See you in the morning." Audi watched her leave through the front door, while Berkley was distracted with her baby doll she left downstairs. She had it swaddled in a blanket with a bottle pressed against the plastic painted lips that did not open.

Audi slowly turned back into the kitchen, and toward Wes. He was still standing by the table, where they both had been *close* just moments ago.

"This is the part where I should probably tell you that I need to head up to my room, maybe call it a night down here and write until the wee hours of the morning…" She was listening intently to him. "But it's only six o'clock…and I really want to finish that bottle of wine." *With you.*

"Oh, you can. I mean, feel free. You don't have to close yourself up in your room. This place is yours to enjoy while you're here. There's the sitting room." She thought of how she needed to clear it of Berkley's toys and dolls. "There's also a sunroom," she pointed beyond the kitchen, "or a gazebo on the grounds if you want to be outside?"

"That all sounds nice," he told her. "I think I will go up to my room for a couple hours to write, and come back down to the sunroom later. Join me for the rest of that wine?" *What did he have to lose? Her husband had run off. He was only going to be there, in the Village of Maryville, for a few days. Any other woman he would have wanted to seduce – and nothing more. But, there hadn't been anyone else quite like her. With Audi, he was drawn to their conversation. He wanted to know more about her. And, yes, he had almost kissed her. Their chemistry was already undeniable. He was inspired, for sure.*

Audi felt her breathing pattern change. *For three days, this man was going to be under her same roof. Suddenly it wasn't Gran's heart she was concerned about. She needed to get a grip.* "Maybe? I'll have to check on Gran, um, that's what I call my grandmother, and get Berkley ready for bed later." *But, yeah, maybe…*

Chapter 5

Audi gathered Berkley and her baby doll from the sitting area, and together they walked up the two flights of stairs to see Gran, who was back in bed. Her wavy white hair was damp and she was wearing a pale pink nightgown underneath the blankets.

The One You're Waiting On

"Did Nurse Jo help you with your shower already?" Sometimes she did, or otherwise Audi would. Gran had one of those modern walk-in bathtub and shower combinations with the nonslip floor. But, she still needed assistance with bathing at this stage in her recovery. Berkley was in the next room gathering her Barbie dolls, as Audi sat in the chair beside Gran's bed.

"Yes, I asked her to. I'm worn out and ready to sleep." Gran said, stifling a yawn. "She worked me pretty hard today."

"That's good," Audi stated, trusting Gran was well on her way to making a full recovery. She had been out of bed in the last twelve hours more than she had in weeks.

"It is," Gran agreed, "now, fill me in on your day here. Berkley told me we have one guest?"

Audi's mind flashed to the image of Wes Delahunt. His charcoal gray *Comfortably Numb* Pink Floyd t-shirt. The way that faded denim snugly fit his lower body. His sandy brown hair. The more she thought about him, the more she felt like she was having a hot flash.

"Yes, a good start for day one," Audi said, pushing away those thoughts that felt forbidden in so many ways. *She was a married woman. But was her husband still committed to her? It sure as hell didn't seem like it.*

"So it all went well?" Gran asked again. "Any flubs that you learned from?"

Audi laughed. "Nope, no flubs. Our first guest is pretty self sufficient." She thought of him eating dinner in the kitchen with Berkley. And then later, pouring himself –and her– a glass of wine. *Wine that he wanted to finish with her later tonight.*

"Okay, well let's hope a few more guests come in this weekend," Gran told her.

"Oh! I didn't tell you. Wes, his name is Wes Delahunt, is staying for three nights."

Gran smiled. "Wonderful."

"Yeah, I know. And…he's a published author. Sort of intriguing…" Audi smiled, and Gran caught a glimpse of something in her eyes. She kept quiet, but she wondered for a moment what was going through Audi's mind.

Gran was tired. Berkley wanted to swing outside before dark. Audi kissed Gran good night, and reminded her again of the bell on her nightstand in case she needed her for any reason at all.

~

Side by side, on the only two swings on that old swingset, Audi pumped her legs with her daughter. They giggled in unison and when the swingset lifted unevenly off the ground, Audi warned, *we are going to tip this thing over!* And they both laughed.

They were stepping onto the front porch when Audi caught a yawn from her daughter. "In the bath now, little lady. It's close to your bedtime."

Berkley scooted off to the private main floor bathroom, which was near the den they were using as a makeshift bedroom. Audi soon heard the pipes knock when Berkley turned on the water. *This old house,* she smiled to herself as she stood at the base of the stairs. She looked up then and she could see the door of the first room on the right, closed. There was light underneath that door. *He was still in his room. Probably working. Writing up a storm.* Audi wondered if he would lose track of time and forget about finishing that bottle of wine. *Probably just as well…*

~

Within minutes after Audi tucked her in, Berkley had fallen asleep. She now had two choices. She could also scoot off to the shower and head to bed? Or she could walk through the main level of the house to be sure the front door was locked, the lights were off…and verify their only guest was in his room.

She kicked off her flip flops in the dark near the foot end of the bed Berkley was sprawled out on. She quietly closed the door to their room and walked across the dimly lit hallway, into the bathroom. She flipped on the light and immediately caught her reflection in the mirror. The loose hairs styled in a bun since this morning were messy tonight, especially after swinging out in the windy air. She pulled her hair completely down and let the wild blonde curls fall. Those locks were untamable for sure. She ran her fingers through them, tucked one side behind her ear and left the bathroom.

The front door was already locked. Nine o'clock was closing time at the inn, and it was now a few minutes before ten. One lamp was lit in the sitting area, and the kitchen light was on. She thought she had turned it off, and only left a dim light on above the cooktop. When Audi walked in there, she glanced into the sunroom first. She saw him, in front of the wall with all windows, sitting on the wicker sofa with fluffy off-white cushions. His focus was on his laptop, resting on his legs. She didn't hesitate to walk in there. The open wine bottle was on the coffee table in front of him and there were two empty glasses beside it.

He looked up and gave a point to the table. "Waiting on you…"

"Pour me one," she told him, and he smiled.

She didn't hesitate to sit down on the sofa near him, but not too close. His laptop was between them on the middle cushion. After she sat, he handed her a full glass of wine and then moved the computer to the coffee table within arms reach in front of them.

She took the glass from him, thanked him, and immediately indulged in a generous sip. He watched her, and suppressed a chuckle. She enjoyed wine. He wondered if she had eaten anything since the last glass she drank in the kitchen.

"How's the writing going since you got here?" The fact that he was a published author continued to intrigue her.

"Really good," he smiled. "This place," from the moment he saw it on the billboard, "inspires me." *And so did the woman seated next to him.* He noticed her curls were down and loose, and he like how defiant they were. Especially the ones that swept over her eye, or touched her cheek. *How damn lucky were those curls...*

"That's wonderful to hear," she expressed, sincerely. "I have to admit, I did think maybe you would lose yourself in writing upstairs in your room and not be down here tonight."

"I invited you. Of course I would show. And yes, I brought my laptop just in case you decided not to join me." He smiled when she laughed. The way she tossed her head back, with her wine glass still in her hand, caught his eye. Her every move, every gesture, captured his attention. He studied people. It was a part of his means to create stories. He tried to figure out precisely what made people tick. It helped when he created fictitious characters in his books. This curiosity, this fascination with Audi, came from so much more. Her beauty caught his attention first, but what he had already uncovered under the surface had just kept getting better.

She leaned back on the sofa and crossed her legs. He noticed she was barefoot, and she had already noticed he had been too. They both were wearing the same clothes they had on all day long.

"How's your Gran?" Wes asked, and she was touched that he remembered.

"She's tired. Her nurse really pushed her today. But, I believe she's getting stronger. I'm so grateful for that. I'm not ready to lose her." That was an admission she had not said aloud to anyone else. But it was heartfelt and true.

"I'm happy her recovery is going well," Wes stated.

"You should meet her while you're here," Audi suggested. "She's quite the character, and she loves knowing she has a guest here. The inn has been her life for so long."

"I'd like that," he said, and he decided to plan on it. But he didn't want to think about his days being numbered to only a few there.

"Do you have family of your own back in Utah?"

"I do. My mother is there, and I have a sister who is married with twin sons. They are two and a half now." Audi watched him smile. She imagined him being a fun uncle.

"No girlfriend awaiting your return?" That was a question that already made her think the wine was talking. Her directness, or maybe it was her curiosity, made him smile.

"No woman in waiting," he said, winking at her. He thought of Pam, the last woman he had a brief affair with. She wasn't interested in having a monogamous relationship and had been upfront about it. They really had nothing in common. Sex and very little communication was the makeup of their relationship, if it could be labeled as one. Wes momentarily thought about how he could talk to Audi all night long on the sofa. His attraction to her was strong, but he had a handle on it. He only wanted to get to know her better. She was married, but who knew for how long? She had baggage…but what a beautiful, spunky little girl Berkley was.

"Waiting," she repeated. "I feel like that's all I've done for weeks….just waiting and wondering if my life as I knew it for so long would ever be the same again."

"Do you want your husband back?" It was a fair question.

"I want my life back, yes. My time here with Gran is only temporary. I want my house in the city, my best friend next door. I want my daughter to sleep in her own bed, but I don't think I can go back to the one I shared with Ben." He now knew her husband's name. "Without an explanation, I have no closure. I have no idea if I want him back. The man I knew and loved would not have done this to me, to Berkley. I'm just really pissed. I was sad, but I've graduated to pissed." She reluctantly smiled, and he chuckled.

"I can't imagine the limbo you're in," he told her. "Life has a funny way of working out sometimes. Just hang in there."

"I have to. For Berkley," she said, sipping more of her wine.

"Yes, and for you," he pointed at her. "Never forget that. You're a mother, sure. But, you're also a woman strong enough to make a life on her own – without a man who's acting like a coward." He had used that word again. And Audi knew he was right. *Ben's actions were cowardly.* "I'm judging your husband and not apologizing for it...I'm sure you're thinking your share about me right now," he presumed.

"I am thinking how my situation seems to really affect you." She believed it cut deep, and wondered if his emotions had anything to do with him only mentioning a mother and sister in his life. And she was right.

"My father left when my sister and I were seven and eight years old." Audi thought of Berkley, even younger at six.

"We were devastated. And I'm certain our mother was too. But she never let us see it. Her strength inspired me, even as a kid. I see some of her in you. I really admire that."

At first, Audi didn't know what to say. And then she spoke exactly how she felt. "I'm really not that strong. Believe me."

"Doesn't matter," he told her. "If those around you perceive it, you're doing something right, and eventually you will believe it."

"That's an interesting way to look at it," she stated.

"It's the truth."

"So your father...he never came back?" Audi wanted to know more. It was someone else's story, it happened at least twenty years ago, but it interested her because her story paralleled it.

"He never came back to us. Not to his wife, nor his kids. He ended up in prison, for drugs, and he's still rotting there." Audi knew that wouldn't be Ben's story. The similarities in the two stories ended there.

"I'm sorry for your pain," she spoke, truly meaning her words.

"Oh it's not so fresh anymore," he replied, "but yours is…and I'm sorry you're hurting." Wes poured the rest of the wine from the bottle into their two glasses. She didn't want to drink the last drop, or end their conversation already. She took a slower first sip this time, and Wes noticed.

"Why did your father leave? Did your mother ever know the reason?" she asked, hoping so. Not knowing *why* Ben left was the absolute worst part of her heartache.

"He didn't love her, or us," Wes began. "He told us so, in a rant, in a ridiculous rage, as he threw all of his belongings into the bed of his pickup. The bastard didn't even have a single suitcase or box. I can still see his clothes and shit flying everywhere."

"That's awful and just cruel, but forgive me when I say at least you knew why." Wes nodded, as if there was no nothing to forgive, as Audi continued. "I've rewound my thoughts a thousand times. Was Ben angry? Distant? Did he still love us?" Audi paused and looked down.

Wes wanted to reach for her hand. One held her wine glass. The other, with that rather large diamond on her finger, rested on her lap. He didn't make the attempt to touch her. He only continued to look at her, and listen.

She let her guard down further with him before she spoke again. "He didn't kiss me," she said, and Wes questioned if he heard her right. "My husband wasn't into that kind of affection. We made love. He touched me, everywhere..." Audi wondered why she was telling him this. She had told no one. Ever. It was something that bothered her, but she kept it to herself. "He kissed my body. He just stopped, over time I guess, kissing my lips. Is that the strangest thing you've ever heard?"

It *was* strange. It was beyond odd that a man wouldn't want to kiss those pink, full lips on this woman. Wes interrupted his own stare at her mouth, those lips that were momentarily slightly parted, to answer her. *So, this Ben guy was stupid too. A stupid coward.* "Damn… as a man who's attracted to beautiful women, I'm beyond puzzled." Audi felt heat on her cheeks as she knew he had just complimented her. *He thought she was beautiful?* She felt disheveled at the end of this day. Wind-blown hair and all. "As a writer, whose focus at times is on a love scene and all its intimate details, I cannot imagine it not beginning with a kiss, a steamy sultry kiss." *Oh my. She really needed to read one of his books.*

"I've never shared that detail with anyone before," she admitted, glumly, and now feeling slightly embarrassed. "Saying it aloud makes it, I don't know, feel like more of a problem than I used to allow myself to believe it was." She marveled now if that was some sort of red flag in their relationship, their union of for better or worse. *Was it her? Was Ben not attracted to her?*

"This is a personal question, so don't answer if you'd rather not," Wes began. This conversation had already turned that corner, and blew past the point of prying in an overstepping or awkward way. They both felt that way. "Did you ever ask him why? As his wife, I imagine you would bring it up." Already he could tell she was a master at open communication. He was drawn to that quality in a woman. And had yet to find it in any woman he was with.

"I did," she was quick to reply. "His answer was first something along the lines of 'I do kiss you…in many different places.'" Wes forced that image from his mind. Her body would be amazing to kiss. *All over.* "And then he told me, almost in a defensive way, that he wasn't any good at it."

The One You're Waiting On

Wes thought of that as a lame excuse and immediately questioned, to himself, if Audi's husband was unsure of his sexuality. But he kept his thought quiet. It was not his place to presume. "Was he, um, not any good at it?" he spoke instead.

"I've kissed a few men in my day," Audi said, almost as if she were teasing him. She took a generous swig from her glass before she continued. "I never compared him to anyone else. When you're in love with someone, you show affection and revel in it without analyzing it, don't you?"

Wes nodded his head. *Jesus. This woman inspired him.* Her mind. Those words that flowed off of her tongue strung together like music. "That makes sense like nothing I've ever heard before. I know you love your husband," he was careful to use the present tense. "I just can't help but wonder something. I'm a man and I'm thinking it..."

"Ben is not gay," she finished his sentence for him. "I'm certain of that."

"I understand," Wes replied, but he really didn't. Probably because he wanted so badly to kiss her for himself. To remind her of what it felt like to be in a lip lock, with tongues exploring and searching for depth. For more of everything. That rush of emotion was proven to spark a release of the oxytocin hormone from the pituitary gland near the base of the brain. Kissing and the release of that hormone increased shared feelings of connectedness.

"I can't believe I just told you that, but honestly it feels pretty good to talk about it. I have fretted about this, especially now that he's gone. Was it me? We shared a physical attraction.

We most definitely did. I just wish he would talk to me. Again, the not knowing why he left has left me with some serious insecurities."

"Don't," he told her. "Don't allow him to do that to you. It's not you. Even if he believed something about your marriage, or you, was not right – that's his issue. Not yours."

"Thank you," she said to him, and she made the first move to touch him. Just the mere brush of her hand on his had sent him reeling. He wondered if she felt it too. That spark that could ignite into a full blown inferno… if they were to fan that flame.

He turned his hand, open palm to hers now, and gently wrapped his fingers around hers. "You're welcome. Please don't let *Ben*," they way he said his name left a bitter taste in his mouth, "make you feel anything less than the amazing woman you are. Yes, we just met. We hardly know each other. I'm not naïve, but I am a pretty damn good judge of character based on first impressions and a little time spent. You are a beautiful, strong woman. You inspire me." There, he said it. She inspired him. Not beyond words though. Quite the opposite actually. An endless multitude of words were filling his mind and flowing off the tips of his fingers. She was a writer's dream. And the answer to a man's prayer.

She giggled. "Well I hope that means you will be able to finish your best-seller after your pit stop in Maryville, Illinois." The idea of him just making a pit stop there, and in her life was a reality. She hadn't dwelled too much on it though. This was only his first night here. Minute by minute, she just wanted to enjoy his company. And *the now* with him.

They released their hands at the same time. "More wine?" she asked him.

"Yeah, I think so."

He watched her walk away. He forced his eyes away from the sway of her bottom. He could see her in the kitchen, moving in front of the refrigerator. *Did this night really have to end?* Another bottle of wine meant it wasn't over yet.

She had uncorked the wine in the kitchen and when she brought the bottle to the coffee table in front of them, he poured it as she sat down again beside him. He noticed she was closer this time. The tightness in his body picked up on that proximity too.

"I'm tipsy," she admitted, with a giggle.

"It's okay, I'll walk you home," he teased, and she laughed out loud. Probably louder than she intended considering her daughter and Gran were both asleep in that big house.

"So what's your plan? To write here, inside of that first room on the right? Or will you be making a trip to St. Louis to dot your i's and cross your t's? "

"That was my initial thought process, yes to go to the city, but my last few trips there have failed me. My publisher is pushing me to meet the deadline this time. I tend to blow past that date marked in red on the calendar, and stall for more time," he explained. *So he was a bit of a procrastinator. Did that mean he also worked well under pressure?* "But, since I arrived here, I'm writing more words than I have in ages. I don't want to jinx it. I'm staying here to write. Bring me my meals to my room and remind me to shower," he teased, and she giggled as she tossed her head back. The way those blonde curls bobbed in place made him grin.

"That really is amazing!" The excitement in her voice was genuine. "I'm happy for you, Wes. And I'm thrilled to know this place, a place I've always believed to be somewhat magical, has inspired you." *Not just this place*, he thought again, and the way she said his name echoed in his ears.

"Audi," he said her name this time, and she liked hearing him say it… as well as the heat she felt in her body, in response. He turned his body further toward her and she carelessly tipped her glass of red wine onto her lap and before she caught her involuntary movement and uprighted the glass again, some of it splashed at her feet onto the hardwood floor.

She gasped, stood up, and moved quickly toward the doorway, muttering about grabbing some paper towels. She was nervous and flustered because she knew what had almost happened between them. Suddenly the weight of her wedding ring felt uncomfortable on her left hand.

"Audi!" She reached the doorway when he said her name again, this time with more intensity. He called her back. He wanted her attention. She spun her body around and her arms were spread wide as her hands gripped onto the door frame. She felt a bit unsteady from the abrupt twirl and the amount wine swirling around in her head. When she turned, he was there. Both of his soft, masculine hands were at the base of her jawline. And he pulled her into a lip lock that began so tenderly she heard herself moan. Her bottom lip, her top lip, one and then the other, were taken so slowly between his. She could feel the tip of his tongue, tasting her. She opened for him, sealed her lips around his, met his tongue with hers. Her arms were still spread wide, her hands white knuckled the doorframe. Her mind was reeling as she was entirely caught up in this kiss. *His kiss. God, this feeling. This moment. Please don't ever let it end.*

Chapter 6

The wine pooled on the floor, and trickled down the side of the glass that she had abruptly placed on the end of the coffee table above the spill.

Her lips felt puffy and were red and throbbing with a pulse all their own. Her hands and her arms had gone limp, falling from the doorframe. She could not get enough of the kissing. His kisses. And he knew that. That was his intention. To make her feel *that* again. The want of someone's lips sealed with hers.

Her senses, every single one, were on high alert. Her body was reacting in every way. The ringing that she heard, however, stopped her instantly. *Gran's bell!*

They both heard it at the same time. It was faint and somewhat in the distance, but consistent. They parted lips and stared at each other. "It's Gran! Her bell. She needs something. I have to go to her." Again, their eyes remained locked. She gently pushed off his chest. *His firm chest.* And backed through the doorframe.

"If you need help," he called after her, "I'm here."

Audi took two steps at a time to get up both flights of stairs. She hurried to open the door and lost hold of the knob as the door bounced off the stopper on the base board at the edge of the wall and beginning of the floor. The heavy wooden door smacked against her shoulder and then ricocheted off. The nightlight plugged into a wall outlet near the bed's headboard kept the room from being completely dark. Audi saw Gran, still in her bed. The blankets on top were disheveled. The white quilt with a colorful pattered stitching, that had turned yellow in spots with time, was half lying on the floor. Gran's knees were up, and she was clenching her chest. "Ca...n't brea...the..." Audi heard her struggle to say.

She immediately flipped on the main light in the bedroom. "Hold on, Gran! I'll call for an ambulance!" As Audi twisted her body back around, she wasn't even through the doorway yet when Wes met her there.

"I've got it," he said, holding his cell phone to his ear. Wes had followed her up there, and waited to be sure everything was okay. But, it wasn't. Gran was in distress.

Audi rushed back to the bed. She grabbed ahold of Gran's hand. "It's going to be all right." Gran nodded, but didn't speak. Audi could see the fear in her eyes as they listened to Wes talk calmly but adamantly into the phone. "We need an ambulance at Besa's Bed & Breakfast in Maryville." He didn't know the street address, but the dispatcher immediately logged it. "An elderly woman, recovering from a heart attack is having trouble breathing…and she has chest pains," he added, taking note of Gran's mannerisms from the doorway where he stood. Audi had tears in her eyes, as she held onto her Gran for dear life.

~

She never left Gran's side. It was Wes who hurried downstairs to turn on the lights, inside of the house and outside on the front porch. He also unlocked the front door for the paramedics before they made their way up the two flights of stairs to Gran's bed. It was then that Audi released Gran's hand, and stepped back. She was trembling when Wes put his arm around her. "It's okay…" he whispered in her ear and she felt tears pooling in her eyes again. The last time Gran had a heart attack, she wasn't alone at the inn and managed to alert one of the guests to call nine-one-one. This time, she rang her bell. *Thank God Audi heard it. She felt a wave of guilt seep through her mind. She should have been in her bed in the den with Berkley, watching the monitor, and listening for Gran. Instead, she was kissing*

The One You're Waiting On

a man she had only known for several hours.

One of the paramedics placed an oxygen mask overtop Gran's nose and mouth. Another stood on the opposite side of her, preparing to insert an IV line. He focused on Gran first, and then on Audi and Wes. "Time is muscle, the faster we can get this treated, the more of the heart we can save. We are giving her medication to speed up her heart rate." With that, the IV was successfully inserted into a protruding vein on Gran's wrist. And then the paramedic spoke to Gran. "Ma'am, we are going to pace your heart just like a pacemaker does." Audi saw some sort of portable heart monitor and heard the terribly slow beeps sounding from it, "and we will get you to the hospital as soon as we can. Okay?"

Gran was coherent. She nodded her head in response. When Audi saw her staring, she pulled away from having the comfort of Wes' arm around her. "I'll need to go to the hospital," she spoke. "I have to get someone to stay with Berkley." She couldn't ask Wes. She barely knew him. She was a better mother than to leave her daughter alone with a stranger – no matter how close she and Wes had started to become. She would have to wake her, or quickly find a trusted neighbor. She even briefly thought of calling Nurse Jo.

Audi didn't have to do either. When Gran was on the gurney and being loaded into the ambulance, three of the neighbors were standing on the front porch. The kind eyes of Colsen's mother, the little boy that Audi had played with a least three times, caught Audi's attention. "Go to the hospital. I'll stay here with Berkley." Her words lifted Audi's worry. She breathed an obvious sigh of relief and reached for her hand. "Thank you. She's asleep on the main floor, in the den. I'll call you as soon as I know something."

Audi got into the ambulance with Gran. She never looked back again after she had seen him walk quickly back into the house. She hoped Wes understood why she did not ask him to stay with her daughter. He hadn't offered. And right now she couldn't think about his feelings. Or her feelings for him. She had to concentrate her full attention on Gran.

~

Anderson Hospital was less than two miles from the inn. The waiting room was half full. Audi found a chair in the corner and sat down. In the ambulance, Gran had stabilized, one of the paramedics shared with her. Now, the doctors would check to see if she, in fact, had another heart attack – and how much damage was done.

Less than five minutes had passed. She was looking down at her feet on the floor when someone approached her a few chairs away. "All is well at the B&B. Berkley's still asleep. I turned off the porch lights and told the neighbor watching Berkley to keep the closed sign out until you return." Wes Delahunt was a godsend.

"Sit," she told him, patting the empty chair beside hers. "I don't even know how to thank you for doing that, and especially for being here." Wes sat down beside her, and leaned into her. His face was close to hers.

"No thanks necessary," he told her, and she gave him a sweet smile. He was relieved to have made it there as quickly as he did. The ambulance had taken off before he had time to follow it, and he wasn't familiar with the area. He had asked one of the concerned neighbors walking away from the inn, where the hospital was located.

"I'm scared for Gran," she said, folding her hands together on her lap. "What is this going to mean for her? We had a good plan in place. She was still able to live at her home, we had Nurse Jo keeping a constant watch all day long. I was just starting to try my hand at running the inn. She appeared to be on the mend." Wes recalled how Audi had just told him that good news hours earlier.

"There is nothing you should have been doing differently," Wes tried to reassure her. "It doesn't matter what room you were in, or what you were doing. You were there for her when she called." Audi wanted to believe he was right.

~

It felt like it had been hours, but it had only been forty minutes of waiting. Wes had encouraged Audi to eat a bag of pretzels he bought at the vending machine, and to drink a bottle of water. When he went to get a cup of coffee, she had told him she didn't drink it. He asked her when the last time she ate anything substantial was, and she admitted at breakfast the day before, as it was now after midnight.

"You're tackling way too much at the inn, as well as taking care of your daughter and your Gran. You need to take care of yourself better. Eat!" Wes scolded her in a playful manner, and she giggled.

"You're not my daddy," she teased.

"I can be your big daddy," he chuckled, and she blushed as she tossed her head back and tried to suppress a loud laugh in public.

"That's the naughty writer in you talking," she stated.

"How do you know?" he asked, happy to see he had averted her attention from worrying about what was happening with her Gran.

She winked at him. "I didn't Google you to read an excerpt, if that's what you're thinking." She hadn't had time. Everything happened so fast. He came to the inn, she enjoyed his company, they were getting to know each other better, and he kissed her. *Well, she kissed him too.*

"One day," he replied, hoping she would read at least one of his books. Her opinion would matter to him more than any five-star rating he'd had thus far.

"I'm keeping you from working," she stated. "You came to this town to finish writing your book and you're spending all of your time with me."

He wasn't complaining. "Something you probably don't know about me is I do what I want to do. I set my own rules. The book will be finished. I have no doubt. It doesn't have to be today."

"Ahh, being your own boss has its perks," she teased, but meant it.

"It does, give or take a publisher trying to breathe down my neck at deadline. But, we all survive once I deliver the story. Right now, I wouldn't be able to concentrate on any story, knowing you were here alone and worried."

"You're doing a pretty good job of calming my worry," she told him.

"Well good," he responded, taking a pretzel out of the bag she had only eaten a few from. He chewed it, while smiling.

~

The pretzels were gone, after Wes pushed her to eat every other one with him. Audi wanted to stand up and stretch her legs, and just as she was about to tell Wes she was going to take a walk to find a restroom, a nurse approached them.

"Are you here for Besa Blackwell?"

"Yes!" Audi stood up, and Wes followed.

"The doctor would like to see you –and your husband too– that's fine," the nurse eyed Wes. They glanced at each other, but did not correct her assumption.

Audi and Wes followed a stocky middle-aged nurse down a short hallway. There, they were met by a doctor. The nurse closed the door behind them before she left.

After the young, almost boyish-looking doctor introduced himself, he told them to have a seat.

"Is my grandmother going to be okay?" Audi wanted to know why she had not been able to see her first. *What did the doctor have to say that could not be said in front of Gran?*

"In time, we hope," the doctor responded. "Her age, and the bradycardia are weighing against her." Audi would explain to Wes later that Gran had a heart condition which produced a slower than normal heart beat. She believed, however, that medication and having Nurse Jo monitor her were both getting Gran well. It may have been naïve of her, but Audi had been questioning why Nurse Jo had not seen any warning signs of a second heart attack coming on. *Weren't medical professionals trained that way?* Audi allowed the doctor to continue speaking. "Your grandmother had a second heart attack tonight. It was slight, but in any case there's more damage. We believe, after running a few tests, that her current medication, administered to slow her heart beat, inevitably slowed it too much." Audi frowned. *What was the point of taking mediation if it was going to worsen the condition?* "I've concluded that your grandmother will need a pacemaker as soon as possible."

"A pacemaker?" Audi asked. That sounded terribly serious. And frightening. Like it was a last attempt at saving Gran's life. *Here, let us place this gadget under the skin of your chest to send electrical signals to your heart, telling it when and how to beat.* That's what Gran needed though. People lived for years with a pacemaker assisting their heart.

"Yes, it's a minor surgical procedure. It will most definitely prolong your grandmother's life. Or, at least it's her best chance."

"Then do it," Audi spoke up.

"Tell that to your grandmother," the doctor replied, with a slight smirk on his face, which had made him appear even younger.

"Oh, so that's why you're telling me, us," she corrected herself as she looked at Wes, "this in private?"

"Talk to her. Stress the importance of this decision – if she wants a few more years of good living."

Audi was in complete agreement with the doctor. When she and Wes walked out of that office, he turned to her. "Go, see your Gran. I'll be here when you're done." He already understood her thinking, and she liked that.

"Thank you," she said, reaching for his hand. She wondered if he felt it, too. The intensity of their connection. The internal heat that one touch generated.

"Good luck," he said, as he slowly let go of her hand and she turned and walked away.

~

Audi stood in front of the closed door to the room she was directed to. She peeked through the vertical rectangular-shaped glass window and she saw Gran in the hospital bed. Audi's mind immediately flashed back to the first heart attack she had. Audi had rushed to this very same hospital as soon as she heard, which was just hours after Gran collapsed at the B&B. Luckily, she had been in the company of one of her guests at the inn at the emergent time.

She pushed open the door, and saw Gran's eyes on her. "Hey Audi girl..." Her voice was weak and raspy, but her words brought a smile to Audi's face. It had been a long time since her Gran called her that.

Audi made her way to Gran's bedside. "What are you doing scaring me like that? You know I can't handle panic scenes." It was true. Audi could barely function when Berkley was learning to ride a bike, had fallen off, and sprained her wrist. She tried to calm her screaming daughter, but the panic on her own face and in her voice had made it worse. Ben had stepped in and saved the day. Audi had nearly lost her mind. If there had been blood, she would have been a goner.

"I think you handled it just fine, sweetie. I noticed you had a little help, too." Gran winked.

"He's our guest, Gran," Audi willed herself not to blush. "He was a great help. He called the ambulance, if you remember." Gran had no idea that Audi had been with Wes when she frantically rang her bell. And Audi wasn't ready to share that with her. The focus had to remain on Gran right now. "We have to talk, Gran."

"About that electronic box that they wanna stuff into my chest? Well they can forget it. I was given one ticker at birth, and that's the one I'll go out with, thank you very much."

Ugh. What a stubborn old woman. "So seventy-eight years it is, huh?" Audi was going to play along.

"I've had a good run," Gran stated, not sure what that even meant. She had already lived two years shy of eighty years old with minimal health issues, yes. But, she had not lived a life without pain. It hadn't been all good.

"Yes, I guess you have, Gran. You've told me about your happy childhood. Then, you fell in love and married a man who gave you a beautiful daughter." Audi thought of her mother. Losing her had almost killed Gran. But, she pulled herself from the rubble and slowly rekindled her spirit. And moved on. "You also have seen much success as a business woman. This town will for sure honor you after you're gone, with a street named Besa Blackwell Boulevard." Audi managed to keep a straight face, and Gran blurted out the first words that came to mind.

"Oh for fuck sake! You know how I feel about that measly gesture!" Gran choked on a cough, and Audi looked at her and winked.

"Just get well, Gran. Do what the doctor is suggesting and add years to your life. I need you. Berkley needs you. You are our family. Please. The inn is not my life. It's yours. Take the steps to get back to it."

"You're a feisty little thing, aren't you?" Gran chided her, as Audi stepped closer and took both of her hands in her own.

"I get it honest," Audi replied, and Gran smirked.

"Should I go find the doctor to see how soon he can wire up your ticker?" Audi held her breath.

"What are you waiting for? Get the hell outta here..." Gran smiled. Audi smiled. *God, she loved this feisty old woman.*

Chapter 7

Audi sat in another waiting area at Anderson Hospital. This one, for family and friends of patients having surgery.

She flipped through a pamphlet Gran had been given yesterday, after she agreed to have a pacemaker. *This procedure does not require open heart surgery.* Audi knew that by now, and was beyond grateful. She read on. *A small incision, approximately five centimeters long, will be made in the upper chest. A lead (thin insulated wire, like a spaghetti noodle) will be guided through the vein into the heart. The surgeon connects the lead to the pacemaker and programs the device. The pacemaker is then inserted beneath the skin. The doctor will test the device for proper function. The incision is then closed.* Now all Audi had to do was wait a few hours for that to happen. And then Gran would be able to resume a healthy, active life again.

She was currently alone in the waiting area. She set the pamphlet aside and gave a few other magazine covers on the wall shelf a once over but didn't take any. She stood up, because she knew she would eventually tire of sitting. She paced the room a bit, just thinking. Berkley was with Colsen and his mother, at their house this time. The inn had been closed for the second day now. And Wes was there with her at the hospital.

She looked up just now as he walked through the doorway. "Found something better than pretzels," he stated, giving her that smile she had gotten so used to seeing the past few days. She noticed he held more than a few white Styrofoam containers. "We have soup, salad, and chicken soft tacos. I wasn't sure what you liked."

"That sounds perfect," she told him, as she pulled up two chairs to a corner table for their lunch.

"And to drink," he said, "we have a choice of Coke or bottled water." Audi laughed out loud as Wes turned around to reveal both of the back pockets of his jeans bulging with drinks.

"Water for me," she said, taking the initiative to retrieve the bottle, nice and slow, from his rear pocket. She took her time and fully enjoyed being that close to him.

"Go on, grab the Coke too," he kidded her, and she laughed out loud. Probably too loud for a hospital waiting area, but she didn't suppress it. And she did take the Coke can from his other pocket. When he turned around, their hands brushed as he reached for his soda. Their eyes met, and their expressions froze. There was mutual contentment on their faces. Whatever was happening, they were allowing it. At least for right now.

"Thank you for being here. For staying. You postponed your trip back home. Not to mention, you have accomplished squat for your story since your first night here."

"How do you know?" he teased her. "I could be writing all night long after I kiss you goodnight at the bottom of the stairwell." He wasn't writing at all, but he had kissed her each night he had stayed at the inn – which was now going on three. Despite their steamy kisses, their growing attraction had not gone any farther.

Audi blushed as she stabbed a forkful of salad and put it in her mouth. Then she politely tried to talk with her mouth full. "I feel bad for distracting you."

"Oh don't..." he groaned. "I'm suffering through it, but I'll make it." She giggled. This, whatever this was between them, was effortless. She tried not to overthink it, and she had not at all prepared herself for the day he would leave to go back to Utah. It would happen though. But, that day wasn't today, so she forced positive thoughts into her mind. Just being with this man, in the moment, was enough.

"Gran was a nervous wreck until they gave her something prior to the anesthesia to relax her," Audi told him. Wes had not gone into Gran's hospital room since she was admitted. There was no need to complicate things. When Gran saw him that night at the inn, in the moment of crisis when she needed an ambulance, she knew of him as just a guest at her B&B. She was grateful for his help during her time of need.

"That's perfectly normal," Wes said, as he took a bite of the chicken soft taco and instantly a third of it was already gone. "Let's hope the procedure goes well and her recovery too."

"She was ready to give up," Audi told him.

"Until you convinced her otherwise."

"I did my best, but it was purely for selfish reasons. Berkley and I need her here. She's the only family we have." Audi was thinking of a few things right now. First, Ben used to be their family. The more time passed, the less likely it was that he would return to them and be that complete family of three again. She also had been thinking so much about her mother. This was the second time in the past couple of days she had mentioned Gran being her and Berkley's only family.

This time, Wes took a chance to see if she was ready to talk about it. "Audi, what happened to your parents?" He had shared with her, the first night they met, how his father left and later ended up as a drug addict serving prison time. His mother and sister were still a very big part of his life. Audi was a little envious of that.

She finished slurping some tomato bisque soup off of her spoon. She should have blown on it first to cool it. Her eyes watered and she reached for a drink. "My mother was Gran's daughter," she clarified for Wes, and he immediately stopped eating and focused on how she had spoken in the past tense. "We lost her when I was twelve years old."

"I'm sorry," he spoke, and maybe it was out of turn. Maybe she had more to say, but first he had to tell her how he felt knowing that she was just a child when her mother died.

Audi nodded her head as she twisted the cap back on her water bottle. "My dad, gosh, this is just really hard for me to say," Audi paused. She guessed it was because most people knew her story, even those she surrounded herself with in St. Louis the past several years. It was difficult to tell someone new what happened. She didn't want her family to be judged again.

"Take your time, or don't tell me now. Wait until you're ready. Things in the past suck to bring up sometimes. I get that."

"Where have you been all my life, Delahunt?" she asked him, not caring how her words truly sounded. *Had she just implied that she needed him?*

He chuckled and went back to eating the rest of his chicken soft taco. He had thought the same of her many times in the past fifty-something hours. "Good to know you're not just using me for my kisses." *Oh those kisses… Had he really any idea what he had given to her? Her insecurity, repeatedly brought on by her husband, had vanished.*

"That too," she added with a lopsided grin.

They ate in silence for a few minutes, and then Audi pushed away the Styrofoam container in front of her. "Yours if you want it," she offered her untouched food to him.

"I'm watching my figure," he said, and she laughed. *He sure was.*

No one was in that waiting room with them. They had at least a couple more hours to wait. Now would be as good a time as any to tell him. "My dad used to physically abuse my mom," she began, and Wes was now finished with his food. That thought sickened him. "She wanted to leave him, but she was afraid of what he would do if he found her, and me. He went too far one night…and I witnessed it." The tears were trickling

The One You're Waiting On

from her eyes as she blinked. "He killed her. Her neck and head injuries were too much. Oh God, Wes…" Audi choked on a sob. *This was old emotion, wasn't it? It had been seventeen years, but time passage didn't matter. She still hurt from it. And now she especially felt more emotional because Gran's life was in jeopardy.* Wes pulled her close, to comfort her. He tightened his arms around her as she cried into his chest. He closed his own eyes. Her pain was now his. There was no other way to describe it. She meant something to him. In such a short time, he had fallen for her.

That son of a bitch. Wes wanted to know what happened to him. *He deserved to burn in hell. But first, someone should have bashed his head in.*

Audi pulled herself out of his arms. His shirt was wet from her tears. She dabbed the tears still damp on her face with a napkin. "I managed to call my grandparents," Audi continued to tell her story. "Grandpa Art was an over-the-road truck driver. Just Gran came. She was the one who told me not to call nine-one-one. She repeatedly told me to call her because twice I had called the police and they always took my dad's side. He had friends on the force. They looked the other way. Gran was tired of it. That time, she came through the front door with one of my grandpa's hunting rifles. It was too late to save my mother, and when she realized that, she told me through gut-wrenching sobs to go into my bedroom and lock the door. I cried. She screamed. I was so frantic I would lose her, too. I should have known better. Gran is super human to me. And always will be." Wes was listening raptly. "Gran shot him, more than once. She killed him for taking her daughter away from her. And I wasn't in my bedroom. I saw the whole thing go down in the living room. In one night, both of my parents were dead."

Audi's father killed her mother, and her grandmother, in turn, killed her father. Wes' eyes were wide and fixed on her. God, this woman had been through pure hell. Unbelievable agony. As a child, she could have been ruined after what she had gone through. Instead, she was the most kind-hearted woman he had ever met. She was perfect in his eyes. The one he was waiting on. He was certain of that now.

"I realize that's a lot to dump on you…but I just thought you needed to know exactly why Gran means the world to me. When my life crumbled as a child, she was there for me. And just weeks ago, I felt the same kind of abandonment from my husband. I packed up my daughter and our life in St. Louis, and I was preparing to run to Gran again – just as she had a health crisis. I've kept myself from crying on her shoulder this time, because she has needed me more. I can be strong for her like she has always been for me. I just can't lose her."

Wes reached for Audi's hand. "She's going to pull through. She's obviously a fighter." Audi smiled at him and nodded her head. "So did your Gran raise you, after your parents…died?"

"Yes, I lived with her and Grandpa Art for six years, and then I went to college at St. Louis University and have been on my own since." Audi sighed a bit, thinking how she had not felt all that independent now, living back under Gran's roof. But, that was only temporary. "Gran was never charged for killing my father. She claimed self defense and that she was protecting me. She was arrested that awful night, but thank God there were no formal charges brought against her. This town really does love her. They rallied for her, knowing she tried to protect her daughter, but was too late. I battled with myself for a long

The One You're Waiting On

time. I should have called Gran sooner, before–"

"Don't," Wes told her, reaching for her again. When he held her, she truly felt as if everything was going to be all right. *With Gran. And her future without Ben.*

"What did you study in college?" he asked her, soon after they pulled apart from their embrace. There was so much he still did not know about her.

"That's a question I always cringe when I have to answer," she replied, and he creased his brow. "I never finished. I spent two years taking basic courses, having no direction and no desire to specialize in anything. I partied with my roomies and then I dropped out. I worked a few jobs – Starbucks, waitressing at restaurants on The Hill, and," she suppressed a giggle, "I was employed for six months at a tattoo parlor."

"You?" Wes chuckled, wondering if under her clothes somewhere she had been inked. The thought made his body tighten in places he had to ignore right now.

"Don't judge me," she teased.

"Oh never," he brushed her off. "I'm just a little taken aback. There's still so much innocence about you that does not match up at all with the things you have told me today."

"Gran had her hands full with me," Audi admitted. "But, then I met Ben…and settled down. And I had a daughter to be a good example for."

"And you are," he reassured her. He did wonder how much control her husband once had over her. Wes already despised that man, and he didn't even know him.

"So," Audi sighed. "I think we need to balance this out a bit. Your turn. Tell me something shocking about you, or your past." She had already known of some of his family's pain.

"Just Google me," he reminded her.

"To find that you are a best-selling author from Utah? That's some serious success to be proud of."

"It is," he nodded. "But we all have reputations. Sometimes people draw conclusions that are spot on. Other times, they couldn't be farther from the truth."

"What's true about you?"

"Here's something I've never told anyone," he began, and she sat back in her chair to listen. "I've been all over this country. I travel looking for inspiration. If I decide the setting of a book is going to be in one particular city, I go there. When I drove into this city," he said, referring to Maryville, "I felt drawn to that massive Victorian-style home. I knew if I ventured by, I would want to go inside. I just had absolutely no clue once I was inside, I would find so much more than a building to fall in love with," he spoke softly, and Audi felt her heartbeat quicken.

"It *is* beautiful, and magical," she had described the inn that way before. She was being so careful with her response. She couldn't jump to conclusions. Living in the moment was what she promised herself she would do. *Look no further, tread without expectations... or you're going to get hurt.*

"The building or this feeling?" he asked her.

"Both," she answered, not taking her eyes off of him.

Chapter 8

A kiss. The way it begins tenderly and escalates with intensity, and finally explodes with want, need, and the desire for more – was addicting for him. *If he had the right woman in his arms.* Ben Pence kissed her as soon as he had her behind closed doors. He had her pinned up against a door at the moment. Her arms were above her head, his fingers intertwined with hers, pressing her body harder against the closed front door of the home he had not lived in for over a month. She moaned when he danced his tongue around hers. He wanted more from her, and she always came through in spades for him.

She could feel him harden through his black dress pants. He was pressing himself against her stomach. He wore a suit again today. She was clad in jeans, sandals, and a white tank top, short of material, leaving her midriff bare. Her long dark hair was down and extremely disheveled at the moment. He stopped kissing her and left her breathless as he knelt down in front of her and glided his tongue over her pierced navel. It was a gold hoop ring, and he stuck his tongue through it. "Uh, so sexy," he said, breathing low on her belly.

"Now," she said… as she unfastened her jeans. He watched her hands. Her seductive hands. She bared herself for him. And then he found her core, as she wanted. He knew what she desired. It had been weeks since the two of them had finally given in to their mounting passion. Sure, he had to leave his wife and daughter in order for her to put out for him. But, *holy hell,* this was worth it. *With the neighbor next door. His wife's best friend.*

She ran her fingers through his short, dark hair, pressing her hands down harder on his head. After she called out his name with her release, he pulled her down on the floor, onto her knees with him, and he kissed her full on the mouth. Having an affair with Phoebe Hunter excited Ben more each time he kissed her.

Oddly, their affair was only a short-term deal. Phoebe's husband worked for the government and was deployed to China for three months. Ben's wife and daughter were living temporarily in Illinois. They both believed their lives would eventually resume without the other. That was the plan. Ben's note said he needed time. Both of them were sure Audi would take him back – and she would never have to know her husband and best friend had been together as lovers. Time and again. What neither of the two expected was the addiction they had for each other. And how damn near impossible it was going to be to part ways.

~

The ringtone of Wes' cell phone interrupted their moment in the hospital waiting room. He looked at the caller ID, and stated that he had to take the call from his publisher.

"Hello!" Wes spoke confidently into his phone. "Dan, my man. How the heck are you?" As Audi sat listening to Wes' side of the phone conversation, she wanted to know more. *What was Wes going to tell his publisher? Was he going to try to buy more time? Or would he be ordered to go back to Utah, or lose his contract?* She knew Wes could not delay publication forever. And she didn't want to be the person standing in the way of his success. He could resent her for it later. Her mind was reeling, and suddenly the familiar face of Nurse Jo peered through the doorway of the waiting room.

As soon as she saw her, and heard Nurse Jo say *–Hi Miss Audi–* she was on her feet. They hugged, and Audi saw tears trickle down her full face with over-applied rouge.

"Awe, none of that, Nurse Jo," Audi nearly begged.

"I can't help it. I already told you on the phone that I feel responsible for not catching it. I swear I listened to her heart rate just minutes before the end of my shift. There had been no change." Nurse Jo wiped away her tears with her chubby fingers.

"I'm not questioning your ability to be a good nurse," Audi told her, honestly. "I've learned it was just a matter of time for Gran's heart to fail her again. The doctor confirmed that. She needs this pacemaker, and I have so much faith in this procedure giving her many more years with me, with us," she said, smiling at Nurse Jo. Her short gray hair was spiked all over her head.

"So I'm not fired?" Her usual stoic expression seemed to have softened.

"Absolutely not. Gran will need you more than ever when she gets out of here."

"That's what I want to talk to you about," Nurse Jo glanced at Wes, sitting against the wall, with his cell phone up to his ear. "I don't want to go out in the hall where we can be overheard, so–"

"He can be trusted," Audi interrupted, to reassure her.

"Okay," Nurse Jo continued, "Dr. Floreza is going to recommend an assisted living center for Besa. Another nurse here told me that he believes she's stressed. Running a B&B at almost eighty years old is too much."

"But, she's not running it. I am, or at least I'm attempting to. We are closed again since I can't be there."

"Audi...I've spent a lot of time upstairs with your grandmother. She worries about what's going on downstairs. She's a perfectionist and no matter who is in charge, it bothers her that she's not able to be."

"Maybe we should move her downstairs, back in the den, so she can see what's going on and be a part of it?" Audi suggested.

"That may make things worse," Nurse Jo offered her opinion.

"So you think she should go to a home? No. I can't, I won't do that to her!" Audi tried to keep her voice down. She could still hear Wes talking into his phone, but she wasn't listening to his specific words. She was too wrapped up in what Nurse Jo was telling her.

"I know how much you love her, honey. I do. Try one week, or two. See what happens. At first, Besa will be defiant, but I know she will come around."

"I don't like this," Audi whined, sounding like a child again.

"No one does, honey," Nurse Jo sighed.

"Well what about you? Where does that leave you?" Audi asked her, because she had hoped Nurse Jo would return to the inn to care for Gran every day.

"That's also why we are talking, honey," Nurse Jo replied. "I have a proposition for you. When I'm not working, I do not get paid. I am a home health nurse. My days of working the floors of a hospital are behind me. I want to take care of your Gran after her possible stay at an assisted living center is completed."

"Of course," Audi didn't think twice. "What will you do in the meantime?" Audi asked, making no secret of knowing Nurse Jo had financial problems. She had implied so herself, and Gran also told Audi about her hardship. Her ex-husband had gambled and lost their life savings two years ago, just when Nurse Jo was on the verge of retiring. He was her husband then, but she had since divorced him when he carelessly lost all of their money.

"I still want to work for you," Nurse Jo stated.

"How so?" Audi asked.

"Let me help you run the inn. Let's get those doors open and keep 'em open!"

Audi didn't know what to say. It was a lot of work for one person, but Gran had trusted her. In addition, Gran never hired outside people to help. "I would have to talk to Gran first." Audi knew they could afford for pay Nurse Jo her regular salary. Gran knew how to save her money. Her bank account was quite comfortable. Audi had been watching her own spending for weeks, but she did continue to share a joint bank account with Ben. That, too, would change soon. Audi was going to hire a lawyer. She had rights, and she was going to exercise them. Maybe it would be a good idea to have Nurse Jo running the inn. Audi needed to get her priorities in order. And move on with her life. She glanced at Wes, doing less talking into this phone and more listening at the moment. He winked at her. She smiled. And then she turned back to Nurse Jo.

"You're hired," Audi told her.

"But what about asking Besa first?"

"I'll make her understand how much I need your help," Audi grinned, and Nurse Jo pulled her into a bear hug. She whispered *thank you*. Audi then asked her if she wanted to stay and wait for Gran to be out of surgery.

"Call me," Nurse Jo said. "I don't want to intrude." She looked over at Wes and then back at Audi. Audi blushed, and Nurse Jo suppressed a giggle on her way out of the hospital waiting room.

Audi turned back toward Wes. He was talking. "Dan, it's a deal. One week and you'll have my story. I owe you. Yes, more than one beer on tap at Shortie's Tavern when I get back." Wes chuckled into the phone and then ended the call.

One week. That's all she had left with him. And it sounded as if he would be spending much of his time working if he was going to finish writing that book, as promised. "Did you just get yourself out of trouble?" Audi asked him, doing her best to act as if this didn't bother her.

"Always," he smiled. "I'll get it done. I'm just going to see if I can rent that first room on the right at the B&B for another week."

"I'll see what I can do to help you with that," she teased. Audi wondered exactly what the next week, their last week together, would bring. She promised herself again to live in the moment.

∼

The following day, the B&B was open with Nurse Jo in charge. Other than Wes upstairs in this room, punching the keys on his laptop, there were no other guests yet. Nurse Jo had agreed to babysit Berkley until the inn was busy. Audi needed her help with Berkley today especially – because she had to be back at the hospital. Gran was going to be released, and Audi had to be the one to tell her she wasn't going home. At least not for two weeks. Audi had already reserved a room for Gran at The Villas in Maryville. The place was just three and a half miles from the inn, and Audi and Berkley would visit daily.

"Hiya Gran," Audi said, making her way into her hospital room. She was sitting up with a breakfast tray in front of her.

"Audi girl... get me the hell outta here."

Audi let out a nervous giggle. "About that, Gran..." Audi sat down on the foot end of her bed. "You need time to recoup, away from the stress of running the inn. Now, before you say anything, I know just being there makes you antsy. You want to be downstairs and have your nose in everything, including who comes and goes."

"So? What's wrong with that? That place is my life."

"I know it is. I get that. I really do, Gran. But, I'm looking out for you, and you need to take care of yourself."

"I swear to God if you send me to a fucking nursing home, I am taking your sorry ass out of my will..." Gran kept her voice calm, but Audi knew she was dead serious. *Well, she may not really remove her only family from her will...*

"It's not a nursing home. It's assisted living. Three point five miles from the inn. The Villas, Gran. Your friend Millie from church loves it there, remember?"

"I need to be at the inn!" Gran was trying her damndest to convince Audi.

"You will be. After fourteen days. Then, Nurse Jo will be taking care of you by day, and I'll be there for you all the time. You're going to be much stronger this time though, you know. You will not be confined to the upstairs."

"Nurse Jo will be coming back?" Audi wondered if she was getting somewhere with Gran. She had not protested being away for only fourteen days.

"Yes, in fact, she's not leaving," Audi knew this could upset Gran. And she contemplated keeping quiet, considering Gran's fragile condition. *Maybe tell her the news about Nurse Jo temporarily helping at the inn after the fact?* "She's helping me with… Berkley. I hired her to babysit, you know, while I'm working."

"Oh, well I'm sure she needs the money," Gran stated. "But, are we really that busy at the inn, where you can't juggle keeping an eye on your own child?" Audi shook her head at Gran's directness. Always saying exactly what she felt, no matter if it was insulting or hurtful.

"It's steady," Audi stretched the truth.

"Is that nice-looking writer still there?"

"Yes," Audi smiled, trying not to allow her entire face to heat up as her insides already had.

"For how much longer?" Gran asked.

"A week. He's writing and that's his deadline before going back to Utah."

"Utah is a long damn way from here," Gran stated.

"It sure is," Audi tried to conceal a disheartened sigh that wanted to be released.

"Tell you what…" Gran offered. "I will go to that godforsaken assisted living center for two weeks, if you promise me one thing."

"Anything, Gran. You know that."

"Don't deny your feelings."

"Excuse me?"

"You heard me. With Ben…that man who never deserved you as his wife… you always gave in. You put him first. Stop doing that. This is *your* life. If you want something, go after it. Others will survive if their needs are not put first. You will be doing us all a favor if you make yourself happy, first and foremost."

Audi was once again blown away by how perceptive Gran was. She knew. For once, she had shown some serious couth. She spoke of, but completely around the subject at hand. She not once mentioned his name. But, Wes Delahunt was someone Gran approved of. And that made Audi smile.

Chapter 9

It took all day to get Gran settled in at The Villas, once she was released from the hospital. Audi had enough clothes already moved there, along with many of Gran's personal items, to make her feel at home. The first thing Gran did was pick up her favorite green plaid fleece throw off the recliner chair and she wrapped it around her shoulders. "A little something from home," she muttered. "Thank you, Audi girl."

Audi sighed. "It's going to be okay, Gran. You'll get stronger every day and be home before you realize that two weeks have passed. I'll visit, and bring Berkley and Nurse Jo."

Gran nodded. "It sucks to get old…"

Audi had never truly thought of her Gran as old, not as in nearing the end of her life. Up until her heart attack, she had tackled life as if she was twenty years younger. "It sucks to be unhealthy, but we're going to get you back to feeling like yourself again."

"I'm pretty good now," Gran stated, "except for I can feel the pacemaker. The doctor said I'll get used to the damn thing. It just seems heavy and feels uncomfortable, especially when I'm laying down."

"Give it time, Gran – and try not to dwell on it." Audi walked over to her and kissed her on the top of her white hair.

"I'll do my best," Gran told her. "Now, you go…I won't worry about the inn as much if I know you're there, taking care of things." Audi had not mentioned that the B&B was open again and Nurse Jo was running it while she was away.

"I'll do that. Call me if you need anything before I come back."

"From what I hear, I'll be waited on hand and foot in this place. Who knows? I may never want to leave…"

"Yeah, right…" Audi laughed as she left.

~

Other than two cars –which were Nurse Jo's and Wes'– it looked like the inn was still vacant. Audi wondered how long it would take for business to pick up and become steady again. Word had gotten around that Gran had another heart attack, and most probably assumed the inn was closed for business again. Audi made a mental note to get the word out there again. *Besa's B&B was open and ready for guests!*

The only guest she really cared about at the moment was the one upstairs writing, Audi presumed, when she walked into the kitchen and found Nurse Jo and Berkley playing cards at the table.

"Mommy!" Berkley called out, taking only a second to glance away from the Old Maid cards in her hand.

"Hiya Berk, are you having fun with Nurse Jo?"

"Oh yeah, we play a lot, since we have no guests. Well, other than Wes the writer." Audi smiled and so did Nurse Jo.

"So is that what our writer is doing now?" Audi asked, trying to be subtle.

"Yes, upstairs still," Nurse Jo stated. "That man really should take a break to eat a meal. Coffee and Coke will hardly keep him alive."

Audi laughed. "I'm sure he'll eat when he's hungry." Audi was just relieved he was able to concentrate and write. She had been a distraction to him since he arrived. *He was distracting for her as well.*

"There's actually a sandwich in the refrigerator that I made for him, and was going to bring upstairs to his door, but we haven't had a break in this card game," Nurse Jo winked, and Audi took the cue.

"I'll deliver that sandwich while you two play," Audi stated, and walked over to the refrigerator.

She climbed the first flight of stairs, carrying a plate with a layered club sandwich on it that she could have sunk her own teeth into.

She knocked once and heard his invitation for her to *come in*. Audi opened the door and saw that his back was to her. He was working on his laptop, which was on a table in front of the window. He had that window wide open, and there was a refreshing spring breeze coming through the screen. That outdoor scent filled the room.

Wes kept punching the keys, because he assumed it was Nurse Jo in his room.

"How's it going?" Audi asked, leaning over him, as her left breast touched his shoulder. She set the sandwich down, next to his laptop. And he stopped typing.

"Oh, hey, you're back...." His body heated having her that close to him.

"Disappointed?" she asked, with a lopsided grin.

"In that sandwich? No way," he teased, licking his lips, and she slapped his shoulder. He tried to grab her hand, but she was quicker and pulled away in time. Then she sat down on the edge of the table, opposite of his laptop and sandwich.

"So, how'd it go with your Gran? Is she all settled?" It

touched her, the way he always asked about the people she cared about.

"Pretty good. Two weeks, that's all she has to spend there."

"She'll adjust, I'm sure," Wes stated. "It has to help her knowing it's only temporary."

"I think that's the only thing keeping her there," Audi replied. "So, how about what's keeping you here? How's that story going?"

"Very well. I can't get enough. My fingers don't move fast enough at times. I'm really happy with the direction I've taken since I arrived here." He meant with his story, but Audi was tempted to read more into his words.

"I'm happy you're happy," she said, smiling, and he reached for her hand. He gripped her wrist and pulled her toward him, onto his lap. He turned around to see if the door to his room was closed. She liked being close to him. Her denim against his. Her body instantly heated.

"I'm known to wait until nighttime to kiss you," he told her.

"Yes, that's your reputation here, Delahunt," she teased him, and did not lean any closer than she already was to him.

"Can we pretend it's dark?" he asked her.

"Oh no…it won't be the same," she told him, keeping a straight face.

"Could be better?" he offered.

"I only came up here to bring you some lunch. Eat. Maybe we can spend a little time together tonight?" Her suggestion made him wonder if she was ready to be with him. He held back, and though it had been pure anguish, he wanted her.

"I'd like that," he said to her, not making a move to touch or kiss her. Having her on his lap was tightening him in places that were obvious already.

"So, I'll go," she said, standing up. He stood up also. He didn't want her to leave, but he had to write. Even still, he couldn't allow her to leave without letting her know how much he had been thinking about her. He already hated being away from her, and it had only been hours.

"Close your eyes," he said, and she did. Her cheeks flushed a bit and she was smiling the whole time.

"Is it dark?" he asked her.

"Uh, huh," she answered, nodding her head with her eyes still closed, as she anticipated what he would do.

"Good," Wes replied, "then this is fair game…" She felt his hands under her jawline. He touched her the same way every time. His lips were soft and she responded. Their tender lip lock quickly turned intense. He met her tongue with his. With force. With a seduction she had never felt previously. *Not with any man before him.*

They both knew they could not do anymore than kiss right now. It was still daylight. Her daughter was downstairs with Nurse Jo. But God, he wanted her. And she believed she wanted him more.

"You're killing me..." she said to him, in between kisses. And she had stolen his very thought.

"Good," he smiled, kissing her harder, thrusting his tongue against hers. "I want you to feel exactly like that when a man kisses you. You deserve to feel that and more." *Just any man?* She caught herself wondering if this was merely his way of showing her that she was desirable enough to kiss. *Maybe that's all this was?* Audi started to question herself, and what they were doing, and Wes felt her pull back.

"I'll understand if you don't want to take this any farther. I know your life is in limbo right now." *Now he didn't want to make love to her? She wanted him to. She was ready to throw away her marriage vows. Ben already had. He continued to hide. Audi had convinced herself that she had nothing to lose. She was ready to be with Wes, completely and without reservations. But, now he wasn't?*

Audi pulled away from him again. Wes assumed he had spoken too soon. Said too much. "I think we need to talk," she stated, not knowing how to begin. He waited for her to continue. "I don't have much of a marriage left. I have no answers. I decided something in the hospital, while waiting on Gran the past couple of days and thinking about how quickly life can change." Wes listened raptly. "I'm going to hire a lawyer. I want to move on with my life. I need to know what my options are in a situation like mine. And, Wes, please know this is not entirely about you. I mean, you have your life in Utah, and mine is here. A couple of kisses are hardly means for a commitment." She was rambling a little, and Wes wondered if she only wanted to *have a little fun with him and then say goodbye?* The thought, even for guy dubbed as a playboy most of his life, shattered him. This wasn't how he perceived her. She was different. He wanted to enjoy every moment of what he hoped they were building together.

They were both misreading each other. Terribly. Audi continued to speak, wishing that Wes would at least say something in response to what she had already said. "I used to live in the moment," she began again. "I want to be that person again."

"Explain that to me, Audi."

"I don't know what is going to happen with my life. I do know that being with you, like this," she said, touching the side of his face with her hand, and taking in that feeling again, "sends me into a tailspin. I like how you make me feel. And, tonight...I want to show you just how much."

Wes didn't even think about it. He just grabbed her, pulled her close, and kissed her full and hard on the mouth. Repeatedly. Until neither one of them could breathe. "To live in the moment sounds pretty damn good to me right now," he said, breathing hard into her neck. He wanted to go farther. He wanted to touch her everywhere. He also wanted to tell her what she really meant to him.

"I'll see you later," she said, going back to his lips for one more kiss. God, how he wanted to do so much more with her. He groaned as she backed away. He couldn't wait much longer to *live in the moment* with her...and now he knew neither could she.

Chapter 10

Audi made her way downstairs. She thought of her husband. With the exception of Berkley mentioning him almost daily, he actually had not crossed her mind much. Not since Wes arrived.

Audi realized what she was feeling was completely crazy. Wes was new and exciting, and the most comfortable, self-assured man she had ever been around. He put her at ease in so many ways. He also fueled a fire in her like she had not felt in forever. If ever. Audi gave herself permission to warrant her own feelings. She was tired of begging her husband for answers. If Ben wanted to contact her, he would have by now. She retrieved her phone from the check-in desk near the front door. She was going to search for a local lawyer. And that's when she heard Berkley squealing. The front windows of the house were open, and the sound of her daughter's glee was coming from outside.

When she walked closer to the windows, she saw Berkley once again swinging as high as she could. Nurse Jo was bending over picking weeds, or something in the yard, a short distance away. Audi smiled, just as the phone in her hand rang. *Phoebe.* Seeing her best friend's name on the caller ID instantly filled Audi's heart with joy. *She missed her. Needed to see her. Be together. Catch up on each other's lives.*

"Hey Phoebs…" Audi spoke into the phone.

"Hey yourself, stranger," Phoebe said, forcing herself to sound as if nothing had changed between them. "How are you holding up?"

"Well…okay considering Gran had another heart attack and underwent the procedure to have a pacemaker put in."

"What? Why didn't you call me?"

"Probably because the past couple of days have been a blur." It was an incredible relief to her, knowing Gran's prognosis was good. "It's best that you're hearing it from me now as I'm no longer panicked. She's recovering in an assisted living center for a couple weeks, and then she'll be back here at the B&B with us."

"So her chances of a full recovery are better because she has a pacemaker?" Phoebe asked, knowing she had heard that before about heart patients.

"Yes, that's what I've learned in the last forty-eight hours." Audi stated. She had never read so much material about the human heart. She wanted to educate herself on Gran's condition, and be realistic about what to expect in her future.

"Well good...and what about you?" Phoebe inquired. She was still concerned about her. Despite the fact that she had blindsided her with betrayal.

"Is this your best friend ESP kicking in again?" Audi laughed, and then she wondered if Phoebe had spotted Ben at the house again, and maybe that was why she called?

"Why do you say that?" Phoebe asked her.

"Something has happened..." Audi began. She didn't want to say that she *met someone*. She was still married after all. And Wes lived halfway across the country. What she did want to say to her most trusted friend in the world was *I'm enjoying my time with this man...and I believe I'm ready to go all the way without overthinking it.* "We have our first guest staying at the inn."

"Well that's wonderful! Is it weird or awkward like you thought, being under the same roof with a stranger?" Phoebe questioned her.

"Not at all. He's a published author from Utah."

"Interesting!"

"Yeah, very. Ever heard of Wes Delahunt?"

"No, I don't think so? I was hoping you were going to say it was Nicholas Sparks!" Phoebe giggled.

"Close...his genre is romance. But Wes is much younger and sexier."

"You can't be serious? Oh my God...get his autograph, or better yet take a selfie with him and send it to me!" *Audi planned on doing much more with him.*

"I'll have to do that before he leaves," Audi smiled again. *Gosh, she was almost giddy.* At a time when the seams of her life were unraveling, she was beginning to feel hopeful that everything would eventually be all right.

"Is he staying more than one night?"

"Yeah, he's already for stayed for a few, and he plans to be here for a week."

"Is he nice? Do you chat with him when you're in the same room?" Phoebe wanted more details.

Yes. He's friendly and so genuine. We've really connected in a way that I don't think either one of us expected. Phoebs..." Audi paused. And then she just decided to say it. She had to tell someone. "We've kissed...more than once."

Phoebe fell silent on the opposite end of the phone. This was the absolute last thing in the world she would have ever expected. *Audi had already given up on her commitment to her husband? Ben's disappearance and lack of communication turned her away and practically pushed her into the arms of another man? Was she rebounding? Was this man using her?* Suddenly, Phoebe had too many questions. This wasn't the plan. *Both she and Ben believed Audi would take him back. She knew he missed his little girl. She thought Audi wanted her husband back because she was lost, lonely and miserable without him. She wanted to see his family reunite. Didn't she?* "You're shitting me, right? You and this famous author are getting it on?"

"Not yet, but close," Audi admitted. *And she wasn't really sure if he was famous.* "Just listen for a second. You know me.

The One You're Waiting On

You know I gave one hundred and ten percent to my marriage. Ben left me. And he has not once answered my pleas to tell me what the hell is going on. I didn't ask for a man to waltz through the front door of the B&B and make my heart do backflips. And he and I are not expecting anything from each other either. We are getting to know each other…and there's this really intense attraction. We want to act on these feelings – and just not concern ourselves with anything or anyone else until we have to, I guess. Jesus. That sounds so reckless and immature," Audi sighed into the phone, as she glanced of the window again to see both Berkley and Nurse Jo swinging. That sight that made her smile.

Phoebe understood more than Audi would ever know. Acting on those pent up feelings, not concerned about anything or anyone, just the moment at hand, was how she had been carrying on with Ben. Phoebe's best friend's estranged husband was her lover. She harbored, but suppressed, tremendous guilt at times. Her remorse was not enough, however, to stop her actions. *Actions that were only supposed to be temporary.*

"Can I say something now?" Phoebe asked her, cautiously, as she nervously ran her fingers through her long dark hair. Thank God Audi could not see the emotional mess she was right now. She couldn't hide the shock she was feeling.

"Yes, but please, don't judge me. I just need to live in the moment." Audi felt as if she was wearing out those words in her mind. "I don't know what's going to happen with my marriage." *She now wanted a lawyer. Ben would eventually have to speak to her. If he wanted out of their marriage, did he also want to leave Berkley fatherless?*

"It's liberating to be in a moment, to be conscious, aware, and in the present with all of your senses. Do not dwell on the past, or worry about the future." Phoebe almost hated herself for making that comment. *Almost.* "Live for now. And call me in the morning with the details!" They both laughed out loud into their phones. But, in the midst of their amusement, Audi heard screaming from the window again. This time it wasn't a delightful squeal. This was the reaction of her daughter crying out in pain.

"I have to go! Berk needs me... I think she's hurt outside!" Audi dropped her phone back on the table and rushed out of the front door, and down the porch steps. Nurse Jo was on her knees, attempting to comfort Berkley. Audi could hear her crying out... *my back hurts, my back...!* She ran to them in the grass, where Berkley was curled up into a fetal position, rocking her body in pain, as tears were pouring out of her eyes.

"What happened!" Audi could hear the panic in her own voice, as she fell to her knees beside her little girl.

"She fell off the swing. She was going too high. She let go and flew out, and went airborne, and then landed on the ground on her back." Nurse Jo appeared calm, but her eyes showed worry. She was a medical professional. Audi made direct eye contact with her for reassurance, for guidance right now. Audi could not handle this kind of panic. Not when it meant her daughter was suffering.

"What do you think?" Audi asked her, questioning without speaking the actual words. *Is anything broken on my child's body?*

"No broken bones," Nurse Jo immediately eased Audi's worry, and momentarily seemed to calm Berkley as well.

"What hurts sweetie?" Audi asked Berkley, making an attempt to move her into a sitting position. If nothing was broken, her daughter should be able to move.

"My back, right here…" she cried, as she turned onto her side again and held her lower back.

"Possibly her tailbone?" Nurse Jo suggested. "She may need an x-ray to be sure, especially since she's unable to move to get herself up."

"I can move," Berkley said, sitting up slowly, "it just hurts here." Nurse Jo now noticed Berkley was moving her hand to an area on her lower back. She quickly ruled out a bruised or broken tailbone because she was seated upright without discomfort at the base of her spine. *Possibly a punctured kidney?* That seemed extreme for a child her age, but not entirely impossible. Children were hardly brittle, but when accidents happened their resilience was amazing. Still, Nurse Jo kept quiet as she encouraged Audi to get her checked out at the hospital. Just to be sure.

~

In the Emergency Room at Anderson Hospital, Berkley's tears were gone, and she was able to sit comfortably in the chair beside Audi. Berkley's ease and constant chatter made Audi wonder with each passing minute why they had come to the ER after all. "So, Berk, is your back better? You don't seem to be in pain anymore."

"It feels sore," she explained.

Audi brushed a little blonde curl away from covering Berkley's eye "Okay. That's why we're here, to get you checked out." She was sure their wait to be seen by a doctor would be longer than the actual amount of time the exam would take. She used Ben's insurance card when they arrived. So much of everything was still joint between them. Ben was Berkley's father. That had not changed. Audi's greatest hope had suddenly become for Ben to still want to be in his little girl's life. She didn't care about herself anymore. If he didn't want her, so be it. She knew all too well, however, what it was like to grow up without parents. Audi thought about attempting to call or text Ben, but as the time passed this appeared not to be a true emergency so she refrained. For now.

Less than an hour later, Berkley was atop an exam table, and Audi stood right beside her. She looked smaller to Audi right now. A little girl with a mop of blonde curls, lying on a sterile hospital gurney. There was fear in her big blue eyes. Audi just wanted to get her out of there, and take her back to their temporary home at the B&B. The doctor asked Berkley to sit upright, and when he pressed his fingers on the left side of her lower back and asked her if it hurt there, she said no. He did the same to the right side and Berkley nearly jumped off of the exam table. Tears sprung to her eyes and she cried out in pain.

Audi felt panic rise in her chest as she tried to soothe Berkley, repeating, *it's okay, you're going to be okay,* and then she stared wide-eyed at the doctor examining her. *Was she going to be okay? What the hell was wrong with her little girl?*

"We will do an x-ray," he suggested. "Could be bruising or a rupture to the kidney. This can be caused by a direct blow to the abdomen, or side, or mid-to-low back. Young people, mainly athletes, can suffer from this. So, we will just take a picture, all right?" The doctor patted Berkley's head, and then looked back at her mother.

As Audi nodded her head, Berkley spoke. "I have to pee, mommy! Can I pee before the picture?"

The doctor smiled. "Let me know if she is unable to urinate. I'll be out in the hall at the nurses' desk, scheduling the x-ray."

Audi agreed, and tried to regulate her own breathing. She needed to hold it together. *It was just a picture. Please God, let her be able to pee. Was that concern she was reading on the doctor's face? Focus. Everything's going to be okay.*

Chapter 11

Audi was able to go along with Berkley to the radiology department to have the x-ray.

The technician placed Berkley flat on her back on top of the x-ray table. When she positioned the x-ray machine over her abdominal area, Audi was asked to back away from her daughter, to protect herself from the radiation. Berkley resisted, but the technician reassured them that it would only take a few minutes. Berkley was told to hold her breath, to prevent a blurred result, as the picture was taken. One additional x-ray was taken of Berkley's right kidney after she was asked to change positions and to roll over onto her left side.

Audi watched a second technician behind a half-wall of glass. He was reading the results and would likely report to the doctor soon. If Berkley had not been within earshot, Audi would have asked if anything alarming showed up on the x-ray. She was confident it had not. This most likely was just a bad bruise on her daughter's internal organ. Audi just needed to be reassured that's all it was.

Berkley looked swallowed up in that open-back hospital gown, as Audi walked with her from the radiology department back to the temporary room in the ER. When they passed a waiting area, Audi instantly caught his eye. Wes was then on his feet and moving quickly toward them.

"Nurse Jo told me what happened. I'm sorry I didn't hear you from my room upstairs," Wes spoke, tousling the curls on Berkley's head. "You okay kiddo?"

"Thanks for coming," Audi said, giving him a grateful smile, but he saw worry in her eyes. "Follow us back, and we'll wait together. Berkley had a picture taken of her kidneys, and we need to talk the doctor about that soon." Wes nodded, and left any other questions he had unsaid. He knew enough not to say too much in front of a child. And her worried mother.

When Berkley settled back onto the gurney, Audi powered on the TV that was mounted on the wall. She found a rerun episode of Full House, and Berkley was instantly glued to it. It was one of her favorite sitcoms to watch.

Wes was standing near Audi when she motioned for him to walk with her over toward the window. "So she fell off the swing?" he kept his voice low. Nurse Jo had fought tears when she explained the accident to him at the B&B. She stayed strong for both Berkley and Audi after it happened, but she felt awful because that sweet little girl had gotten hurt on her watch.

"She always swings high. She's big enough to hold on. I don't know exactly how it happened. That old swingset has never been anchored into the ground. It doesn't matter now. I just need her to be okay," Audi whispered.

"Why the x-ray of her kidneys?" Wes asked.

"That's where the pain is...and before the x-ray, she had trouble peeing. She feels like she has to go, but can't," Audi sighed, and Wes saw tears pooling in her eyes. She immediately batted her eyelashes, forcing back her emotion. She wouldn't let Berkley see her upset.

Wes took both of her hands in his. "I'm here for you both," he said, sincerely.

"Thank you..." Audi began, "but this is the second time you've followed me to the hospital in less than a week. You really need to focus on why you stopped in this town to begin with." She was referring to his writing, and he smiled at her.

"I am focused on where I want to be and who I want to be with," he told her, still holding her hands in his. "In such a short amount of time, you have come to mean so much to—"

The doctor, who both Audi and Berkley recognized from earlier, knocked twice on the doorframe as he walked into the room. Wes immediately let go of Audi and she walked over to sit alongside of her daughter on the bed.

"Hello pretty little lady," the middle-aged doctor with olive skin coloring and thick dark hair, walked over to the bedside and stood close. Berkley's attention remained on the television, and the doctor caught Audi's eye. "Could we talk for a minute?"

"Berk, um, just keep watching your show. I'll be right back." Berkley barely nodded her head and never looked away from the screen. Wes took two steps forward. *Should he stay with Berkley? Or go with Audi? Who would need him more?*

The One You're Waiting On

Audi turned to him and reached out her hand. "Come," was all she said. And he was so relieved she wanted him by her side. He didn't have a good feeling about the doctor wanting to speak to her without Berkley present.

Just across the hallway, the doctor closed the sliding glass door to the vacant cubicle in the ER, and then he closed a privacy curtain over it. It wasn't a private office, but for the moment he was using it as one. Audi stood close to Wes, waiting for the doctor to speak.

"Let me start by saying the x-ray did show an inflamed kidney." *Inflamed? Did that mean bruised as he originally thought?* Audi's clammy hands began to tremble. She took a deep breath in an attempt to calm her nerves. "Sometimes accidents happen and are seen as blessings in disguise." Audi didn't understand where the doctor was going with this. She just wanted to know. *And she wanted to know now. What was going on with her little girl?* "We detected a mass on your daughter's kidney..." Wes immediately put his arm around Audi. He squeezed her shoulder tightly, and felt her fall into him. Audi could not handle this kind of panic. He used additional strength to hold her upright. "We're turning this over to a specialist, here in our hospital, because a biopsy is needed to see what we're dealing with."

Audi covered her mouth with her hand, as the tears sprung to her eyes, and this time she didn't force them back. "Oh God...no. A mass? As in a tumor? As in something that could be cancerous?"

"We don't know for sure," the doctor's voice was calm and almost soothing. But Audi wasn't interested in being calmed or soothed. *She wanted to know why her daughter had something foreign growing on one of her most important internal organs!* "They'll do the biopsy in a few minutes."

"Okay, wait! Just wait!" Audi raised her voice. "What do I tell her? How is this biopsy done? Will she be awake during this? Can I be with her?"

"A long needle will be inserted through her back to retrieve a sample of the mass to send to the lab," the doctor remained professional, but Wes could see the compassion in his eyes. Speaking to a worried mother of a child that could be seriously ill was not an easy task. *If you're human, you feel each other's pain.*

Audi was crying again, and she nodded her head when the doctor said she could stay with Berkley during the procedure, to help keep her calm. That was going to be one hell of a task when Audi was currently having an incredibly difficult time holding her own.

The doctor left the room, after telling both Audi and Wes that they could take a moment in there to pull themselves together before going back across the hall.

The door wasn't closed yet, and Wes had already pulled Audi into his arms. She let go and sobbed into his neck. He stroked her hair, rubbed her back, and just allowed her to feel. She needed to let this out – before returning to her daughter, where she would have to be strong again.

Wes wished he could reassure her. He wanted to say the words, *it's going to be okay.* But he couldn't. Because right now, no one knew for sure.

Chapter 12

Audi sat at the bedside of her sleeping daughter. She was now an official hospital patient, admitted and given a private room. At least until the doctor had some answers. The lights were off in one half of the room, but Audi was still focused on, and able to clearly see, her little girl. Her chest was rising and falling. She was calm at last.

The procedure was traumatic for her. Berkley couldn't get past the fact that they put a needle in her back. It stung before the numbing medication took effect. She cried. She fought. Finally, Audi was able to calm her, speaking softly and closely, with her lips against her ear. Their faces touched until it was over and their tears crossed paths rolling down each other's cheeks. While Berkley was the one physically enduring this, Audi suffered more. Just watching. And knowing. Was excruciating.

The door opened slowly, and Wes walked in, making a conscious effort to be quiet. Audi had asked the nurse to tell him the procedure was over. She didn't look up as he stood closely behind her and placed his hand gently on her shoulder. She reached for him, touched his hand with her own, but never turned around. When she bowed her head, Wes knew she was crying.

She abruptly stopped herself short of feeling, stood up, and walked across the room to be near a window again. Wes followed her. "How long until you know?" he asked, referring to the results.

"An hour or so. Berkley should sleep that long. They medicated her. There's going to be some pain or discomfort when she wakes up. She just needs to relax for awhile."

Poor girl. And her poor mama. "I'm sorry this is happening." Wes didn't have the words to fix this, but he wished he did.

"Me too," Audi sighed. "It just feels surreal, you know? I'm asking myself how did we get here? How did she go from happy and healthy, squealing on the swing, to having a needle prodded into her back...looking for...cancer?" The word sickened her and could easily break her. *It would, Audi knew, if this nightmare didn't end with positive results today.*

"Don't give up hope," he told her, realizing she may already have known something. A mother's intuition was spot on.

"I'm scared out of my mind. I'm not strong enough for this. I'm not!" Wes pulled her close and tightened his arms around her. He spoke through the soft blonde curls covering her ear. "You don't have to do this all by yourself. Feel this," he said tightening his arms further around her body. "That's my strength...and I'm going to use it hold you up through this." That did it. His words. His unwavering support since the moment she met him. All of it made her openly release her overwhelming emotions, as she sobbed in his arms.

It wasn't fair to expect anything of him. In less than a week, Wes had a home to go back to. And Audi knew she needed to contact Ben. He had a right to know what was going on with their daughter. She would leave him a message. But that would be all. She would not chase him down, or beg for him to be there for their little girl. She feared the worst right now, and had shut out everyone around her. It was a reaction that stemmed from panic. She remembered doing the same when her parents died. And then, it was Gran who, in time, managed to reach her. *Gran. Audi needed her so badly right now. But she couldn't go to her. Not yet.*

Wes held her in front of the window in silence. He was careful not to push her. Not now. Not when she was so fragile. But he wanted to be there for her – and for Berkley. He wanted that more than he'd ever wanted anything before.

The door opened slowly. The shift must have changed because Audi did not recognize the nurse. "Hi," she kept her voice low after glancing over at Berkley, asleep on the bed. "I'll stay with your little girl for a few minutes. Dr. Barnes would like to see you in his office." He was the specialist who had taken over Berkley's case. It terrified Audi to think she even had a case. Audi looked at Wes. He reached for her hand. She accepted it, and probably clenched his fingers tighter than she realized. She looked over at Berkley, asleep in a hospital bed that practically swallowed her up. *I'll be right back, baby girl. Everything is going to be okay.*

∼

Dr. Barnes remained seated behind his desk. Audi led the way into the room. It was just too quiet. It wasn't awkward silence. It was worrisome. She and Wes sat down in the two chairs, side by side, in front of the large cherrywood desk. The doctor, who looked seasoned and probably close to retirement, sat with his hands folded on the desktop in front of him. Audi never spoke a word. She just sat there and waited to hear the news.

Sometimes it's better to just speak. Say what you have to say. And get it over with. And then, one of the two would follow – either relief or fallout. "The x-ray showed a mass on your daughter's kidney, and unfortunately the biopsy was conclusive…it's cancer." If Audi had been standing, her knees would have buckled and her body would have collapsed onto the floor beneath her. Her hands, one clenched to the other as if she was in the midst of a desperate prayer, trembled and Wes grabbed her firmly around the shoulders with a strong, comforting arm. Tears filled her eyes, but she was afraid to move. Just one blink, and the floodgates would open and she'd never be able to stop. *Breathe. Listen. Regain control. You are her mother. She needs you. God help me. God save her. Please.* "I'm confident, but not certain that the cancer is confined to the mass on the one kidney. We will need to run further tests, an MRI to be certain. And surgery to remove part of, or possibly your daughter's entire kidney, will have to happen promptly."

"So...the other one, um, Berkley's other kidney...it's alright? It's normal and healthy, and she will be able to live with just one kidney? I mean, people do it, right? You will remove the cancer, and possibly the entire kidney, and my little girl will survive this, correct?" Audi was nervously rambling. It was as if her words were frantic pleas.

"We most certainly can live with just one kidney. I have no reason to believe that her other kidney is not healthy. We will run further tests. Unfortunately I will not know, until I operate, whether or not her entire kidney will need to be removed. My main concern is ridding her body of the growing cancer. Just taking the mass could leave a trace for the cells to grow again. I'm just preparing you for what may need to be done."

Audi nodded her head, and inhaled a deep breath. "How soon are these tests? And the surgery? I need to prepare her. I need to talk to her and help her to understand what will be happening. She's only six years old," Audi choked on a sob, and then stopped talking.

"I understand. Go talk to her. We will schedule the MRI today...and the surgery in a day or two. No more than that. I want to act fast." The doctor wanted to immediately rid the little girl's body of that awful disease. He had seen too much of it in his career. It was sickening and unfair. With each and every case, he fought his patient's battles right along with them. This little girl, with those soft blonde curls and blue eyes, touched him beyond words. And her mother's pain right now was slowly chipping away at his soul.

Audi stood up and Wes followed her out of the office. She heard him say thank you to Dr. Barnes, but she had just kept walking. *She would thank him when he saved her little girl's life.*

In the hallway, just outside of Berkley's room, Audi stopped walking and turned to Wes. He was standing there, wide-eyed, and ready to help with anything. This, however, Audi needed to do alone. "I'm going to text Ben. He needs to know what's going on. He will get one message from me, and that is all." Wes knew Audi was finished with being ignored, but he admired her for not shutting him out of this crisis with their daughter. This woman in front of him, this woman he wanted beside him, amazed him. And more.

Wes nodded his head, and said, "Okay. What do you need from me?" She stared at him for a long moment, standing there in his faded jeans with the hole in one knee, and that charcoal gray Pink Floyd t-shirt that read, *Comfortably Numb* across the front. Those were the clothes she had first seen him in when he arrived at the B&B. He was repeating the wear of his clothing because he had only packed enough for a few-day stay. So much had happened in such a short amount of time.

Audi's eyes were pained, but she gave him a sweet lopsided smile with her lips sealed together. "Go back to the B&B. Tell Nurse Jo what's going on. I know I need to be the one to tell Gran, but I'm just not ready yet."

"Do you need me here, when you go in there?" he asked, referring to the moment when she had to tell Berkley that her time in the hospital, where she justifiably wanted so badly to leave, was just beginning.

"I do, but I don't," Audi attempted to answer. "I have to do this alone."

"I understand..." he replied. "Give me your phone."

"What?" as she questioned him, she reached into the front pocked of her comfortable flared jeans that hugged her narrow hips and shapely backside just right.

"I'm going to plug my number into your phone. We haven't done that yet." Audi smiled at him again, this time her pearly whites showed. "If you need me for anything while I step away, call me, and I will be right back here so fast your head will spin."

She suppressed giggled because, *Lord have mercy, her head was already spinning. For so many reasons.* When he gave her phone back, their hands brushed against each other's. He grabbed her by the wrist and pulled her close to him. With her in his arms, he spoke softly into her ear. "The last thing you need is for me to add to your roller coaster of emotions, but just know you can count on me. You can be honest with me. Tell me how you feel. You will not scare me off."

"How I feel?" she asked him, almost at a loss for the words to explain. She was still standing close enough to him to touch his chest. She softly traced one finger on the lettering of his shirt. "I wish I was comfortably numb."

He smiled. She smiled. And then he quoted the song they obviously both were familiar with. "Is there anybody in there? Just nod if you can hear me… I hear you're feeling down. Well I can ease your pain. Get you on your feet again."

She nodded her head – with tears pooling in her eyes.

Chapter 13

She sent him a text. All it stated was *Berkley's in Anderson Hospital in Maryville. It's serious.*

She also replied to two somewhat frantic texts from Phoebe, both of which had been sent hours ago. *Berkley's in the hospital. A fall from a swing led to an x-ray of her kidneys. It's bad, Phoebs. My little girl has a mass on her kidney. It's cancer. I can't talk now. Don't call. I texted Ben. Who knows if he'll respond? I'm scared to death that I'm going to lose her. I'm sorry, but I have to go.*

Audi was at Berkley's bedside when she opened her eyes. The medication had worn off, and she looked completely relaxed. Until she moved. The discomfort of having a needle in her back during the biopsy would remain for a few days, the doctor had said. "Mommy, it hurts," Berkley instantly broke into tears.

"I know, honey. I'll get the nurse in here to give you some medicine for the pain."

"No more medicine!" she wailed.

"Okay, okay... shhh... just be still. Find a good comfortable spot and don't move your body." Berkley did as she suggested.

"I want to go home," Berkley said in almost a whisper.

"I know, me too," Audi agreed.

"No, I mean home! Back to St. Louis, where daddy and my friends are. I'm tired of living at the B&B." Audi was taken aback by her child's honest words. But, why should she have been? Home was in St. Louis, and to Berkley, her daddy was still very much a part of their family. She enjoyed Nurse Jo's company and loved Gran – but Gran had disappeared from her life, too, as she now was living apart from them. Even if it was only temporary, a six year old couldn't fathom that.

"Let's just get you better first," Audi replied thinking, *and then we will figure out where our home is.*

"Do I have to stay here to get better?" It was a simple, direct question, and Audi could hardly find the words to answer it. But she had to. There had been no response to her

The One You're Waiting On

message to Ben. He had abandoned them. Audi was the only one her daughter could count on now. She had to come through for her.

"For a little while, yes. Your kidney is sick. We all have two kidneys in our bodies, and one of yours needs some work done on it to feel better and be healthy again. It's no trouble for your other kidney, the good one, to take over and do the job of both kidneys."

"What's going to happen to my bad kidney?"

"Well, there's a sore on it right now and the doctor wants to take it off."

"So he's going to cut me…with a knife to get inside of me and then cut me some more to take the bad part of my kidney out?" *In a sense, yes. Exactly.* Audi kept her emotions in check, but *God how she wished this was her, instead of Berkley.*

"Yes, you are going to have surgery," Audi refrained from telling her about the possibility of the doctor having to remove the entire kidney. There was no need to go into that detail. It was entirely too much for a six year old. It was too much for her mother, too.

"Gran had surgery to make her better. Am I going to be the same way after I'm cut?"

"Yes, baby girl, yes." It was an answer that Audi chose to believe with all of her heart.

~

Less than one hour later, the door to Berkley's hospital room opened. She expected to see a nurse, or maybe even Wes. *Hopefully Wes.* She knew he would come back after he talked to Nurse Jo at the B&B. But when Audi looked up, she saw Phoebe, stationary in the doorway. Her dark hair was pulled back into a low ponytail. Her eyes were wide. She never failed to look completely put together. Her hair, her midi dress, her ankle wrap wedges. Her appearance was a far contrast to Audi's right now, in jeans and a pale yellow v-neck t-shirt with flip flops on her feet. Audi stood up. Phoebe took quick steps toward her. Audi moved just as promptly to meet her halfway. They embraced intimately and tightly, and both tried terribly hard not to cry, because Berkley was watching them closely.

"Thank you for coming...God, I've missed you." Audi words were honest and true. Phoebe closed her eyes – forcing away her guilt – before they pulled out of their embrace that lingered.

"I'm here for you. Always," Phoebe said, now looking over at Berkley. "Hey kiddo. How are you feeling?"

"Sore, but the nurse gives me stuff for the hurt in my back, where they put a long needle in me. My kidney is sick."

"I know, honey..." Phoebe said, walking over to her bedside and kissing her on top of the mop of blonde curls.

"Have you seen my daddy?" Berkley spit that question out so fast that it took both Phoebe and Audi by surprise. *Phoebe more so, however, because she had.* They both realized it was an innocent question, considering they were neighbors.

The One You're Waiting On

"I have," Phoebe answered, as Audi spun her head around to look at her. *She had?* "He will be here soon. He's on his way now." *He was?* Suddenly Audi could not handle that thought. *Ben would be there in the same room with them? And she was expected to act as if he had never left?* Deep down in her broken heart, she didn't believe he would respond to her text, let alone show up there.

Phoebe was watching Audi's face. She wasn't the only one who was going to feel incredibly awkward when Ben walked into that room. Audi had texted them both, just minutes apart. They were together. Ben was frantic, and guilt ridden when the text Phoebe received revealed everything that was going on. His text from Audi had been vague. Phoebe had never seen Ben that way. He lashed out at her. Out of fear. Out of guilt. And then he apologized. Phoebe understood how upset he was. She followed him in her car to the hospital. He was waiting in his car in the parking lot right now. She told him to allow her to go in first. It was killing him. He wanted to get inside to his little girl and find out what was happening. But, Phoebe believed her entrance first, and the chance to warn Audi that he was coming, was best.

"Oh good! My daddy is coming!" This was the happiest Audi had seen Berkley in several hours. She, of course, loved Ben. And she missed him. Audi didn't want to believe he would ever let them down, but he had. And now that her trust was completely shattered, Audi dreaded the moment she'd see him again. *How would she pretend in front of their daughter that everything between them was just fine? That nothing had changed. When, in fact, everything had.* She momentarily thought of Wes. And then, when she looked over at the doorway, she saw Ben standing there.

Chapter 14

His dark hair looked shorter, like he had just gotten a haircut. She assumed he was back to work, *no more leave of absence*, and he must have come there straight from the office as he was still wearing his dark suit, sans a tie. Audi didn't stare, but she did look at him long enough to realize he was really there. It unnerved her that she felt a little bit of comfort now, knowing she was not alone in parenting Berkley through this nightmare.

"Hiya Berk," Ben said, addressing only his daughter. Phoebe refrained from making eye contact with him, and looked across the bed at Audi. This feeling of being in the middle, *being the other woman who was sleeping with her best friend's husband,* was threatening to overwhelm her at the moment. She focused on Berkley, and then she felt worse about herself knowing she was the reason this little girl may never have her parents together again. *It was supposed to be an affair. Just a fling. Something no one would ever know about. And then they all would resume their lives.*

"Daddy!" Any soreness from the biopsy was not evident at the moment as Berkley pounced up on her knees on the bed and threw herself into Ben's arms.

"I missed you like crazy," Audi heard him say. She turned her head away from them. *How could he have left them? Left their sweet Berkley?*

Audi didn't say a word, she just walked to the foot end of the bed and then glanced at Phoebe, who she knew was staring at her.

"So, are you feeling okay?" Ben asked as he held his daughter in his arms. He ached from the pit of his stomach up to his throat. It made him physically ill to know his little girl was going to have to battle cancer.

"Uh huh," Berkley nodded her head, and then Ben looked at Audi. It was the first time he had really stared since he walked in. It was difficult for him to face her. He noticed her blonde curls were more disheveled on her head. Her blue eyes were tired and red. The stress and the tears had already taken a toll. Her tiny figure had not changed a bit, or maybe she had lost a little weight. But she still looked beautiful to him. *Had he ever told her that?*

"We're staying overnight here for a few tests, and then either tomorrow or the following day, Berkley will have surgery to heal her kidney," Audi spoke in terms that her daughter would understand. She could hardly make eye contact with her husband while she did though. She never thought the first time she saw him again, after he abandoned them, that their conversation would go like this. She imagined demanding answers as to *where the hell he'd been, and what he wanted from her and from their marriage. Did he want out? She did now.*

"And then you'll be as good as new again!" Ben tried to keep the mood light and his little girl's spirits up. She giggled as he gently pinched her nose.

"And then we can all go home together to St. Louis!" Berkley exclaimed, and Audi looked away. She didn't want to see Ben's face, or hear what he had to say to that notion.

"Hey Berkley...what do you say you and I take a walk down to the gift shop to see what kind of stuffed animals are in there? Can she leave for a bit?" Phoebe asked, and both Audi and Ben knew what she was doing. They needed to talk.

"Yes, that's fine," Audi smiled softly at Phoebe. Ben squeezed his little girl one more time and then put her down on her feet. In her hospital gown and slippers, Berkley walked hand-in-hand with Phoebe.

When the door closed, Audi crossed her arms over her chest and glared at her husband. "Where the fuck have you been?"

His eyes, fixated on her, did not change. He didn't look uncomfortable or nervous. "I told you I needed time."

"To do what? Fuck around on me?"

"What's with your language?" He was used to the foul mouth from Phoebe – she was fire and ice – and the indecency of that and everything else about her turned him on. But, for his wife, this was a little new.

"I'm angry. I'm hurt. And, quite frankly, I feel done with you – and with us. But, here I am, forced to see you and speak to you because our daughter is sick." Audi choked on a sob.

"I can't believe this," he shook his head, choosing to focus only on their daughter rather than how he wasn't ready to give an explanation or an excuse for why he left and why he ignored every single one of her messages.

"Believe it," she said throwing her hands up in the air. "Look around. We are in this hospital because our little girl is sick. She could lose her entire kidney because of the mass of cancer growing on it."

"What? Are you serious? What does that mean, I mean, can she live with just one kidney? People do, don't they?"

"People do, yes. I don't have the answers. The doctor will not know anything until he operates."

"Will she, um, have to have chemo or radiation?"

"Please Ben, don't. Pray to God the surgery takes care of the cancer. Tests are going to be done today yet to see if it's anywhere else in her body." Tears pooled in her eyes. This sickened her to no end. She stopped talking and walked over to the window. Ben remained standing where he was, now across the room from her. She wanted distance between them, and he wasn't going to push.

"I'm sorry," he spoke softly, almost too quietly, but she heard him.

"You should be," she spoke immediately after his apology, which she didn't even care if it was sincere or not.

"So, where do we go from here?" he asked, wondering that exact same thing now more than ever. His affair with Phoebe would have to end. Now. *Did he want to recommit to his marriage? Did Audi?*

"We?" she asked him, and her voice was cold and heartless. "The only thing we are going to do together is be present for our daughter. That is, unless you decide to bolt again? She thought you were working. I never told her otherwise. That's why she still wants to see you and be with you. I, on the other hand, think you should go to hell!"

He wondered about this change in her. All of her messages had been pleas. *She couldn't live without him. She loved him. Please come back.* And then her attempts to reach him had completely ceased. And now, there was a strength he had never witnessed in her before. She was hurt and angry, but there was something more. "I don't want to fight with you. Not here. Not now. I love our daughter just as much as you do."

"Stop!" she called him out. "I don't have it in me to abandon her like you did, so do not compare my love for her with yours. You have a strange way of expressing your kind of love."

He deserved that. And, as he stood there now, in the same room with his wife after weeks of hiding from her, he wondered if it was worth it to him now. There was no way Phoebe would ever leave her husband, she had already made that clear. And the wife Ben believed would take him back, had changed. She hated him now. Or, hated what he had done so much that she no longer wanted him. And she didn't even know the truth about where he had been. And *who* he was sleeping with.

"I'm staying here for the tests," he told her, almost as if he wanted to reassure her that he was done running.

"Fine," she answered, and turned her body to look out of the window. Without facing him, she asked again, "Where were you?"

As if it were easier to talk to her back, to not have to look at her face and see the disappointment in her eyes, Ben thought he could find the courage to speak openly this time, to tell her *there was someone else.*

Audi closed her eyes for a moment, and inhaled a deep breath. "Are you having an affair?" His answer should not have come as a surprise to her, but she still felt a pang of terrible hurt in her heart when she heard him say *yes* from across the room. "So, a coward's way was to say you needed time and run away? For how long, Ben? Have you gone from her bed to mine? Have you kissed *her* on the lips?" Audi had instantly gone from hurt to furious, and everything she said to him caused Ben to feel flustered. *He was a grown man. He didn't have to answer to anyone.*

Before he could reply, not that he intended to be honest, the door opened up and Berkley walked in struggling to carry an oversized stuffed elephant. Phoebe was behind her, helping, and the smile on her face quickly faded when she sensed the intense moment they had interrupted.

Berkley showed off her stuffed elephant, one she could barely lift up onto the bed, as Ben assisted her. Audi smiled sincerely at her daughter. Before any of them spoke to each other, in the midst of Berkley's chatter, the nurse walked into the room. "We are ready for your MRI, young lady."

"What's an NRI?" Berkley misunderstood, and looked to her mother for an explanation.

"Just more pictures. Can I go along?" Audi asked the nurse.

"Not for this one, but your elephant can go with us," the nurse said, feigning a struggle to pick it up off of the bed and Berkley giggled. She seemed okay with having to leave the room alone with the nurse, so Audi walked over to her first. She bent down on her knees, kissed Berkley's cheeks one by one, and then gently squeezed her. "I love you more than anything. Be a good girl, do what this kind nurse and the other technicians tell you. And I will see you very soon."

Ben gave his little girl a quick squeeze, as Phoebe stood back and watched the scene again. And when the door closed, it was Phoebe who spoke first. "I should go," she offered, in what Audi thought was an attempt to leave the two of them alone again to talk privately.

"Oh honey, you don't have to leave. He and I have said all there is to say." Audi never looked at Ben, and when Phoebe did, he lifted his eyebrows at her and shrugged his shoulders.

Audi went to Phoebe this time, with her arms open. They held each other for the longest time, as Ben looked on. The friendship, the bond between those two women was special. And now, what he and Phoebe had done, was sure to destroy it. If the truth were to ever come out.

"Berkley's going to be okay, isn't she?" Phoebe still needed answers.

"She has to be," Audi responded. "If something happens to her, I'm done. I'm done with this thing called life." Ben stared. Phoebe ran her hands through the curls near Audi's face.

"Shh. Stop. Your little girl is going to be just fine."

Ben left the room when they were talking. He muttered something about *going to see if he could get a cup of coffee.*

When he was gone, Audi spoke first. "He's cheating on me."

"He admitted to an affair?" Phoebe asked, feeling incredibly awkward. But not all that guilt ridden.

"Yes, the bastard! How could he?"

"Well, Audi, please don't get pissed at me…but the last phone conversation we had, you told me you were attracted to and kissing that sexy author at the B&B."

Audi eyes widened and she immediately defended herself. "That's unfair! Ben had already left me."

"I'm not implying that it's the same thing…I'm just pointing out that attractions to other people do happen in a marriage."

"So it's okay that my husband has been cheating on me with who knows what kind of floozy?"

Phoebe cringed. "It's not okay, but just think about how the two of you have grown apart. Be open-minded."

"Grown apart? He just up and left me! I cannot believe you are telling me this!" Audi was angry. "You're my best friend, you're supposed to be on my side!"

"I am on your side. I'm also in Berkley's corner. You and Ben need to set aside your issues for her. She needs you both more than ever."

Audi sighed, willing herself to calm down. "I know you're right. I don't care who Ben's been with. I just want him out of my life…but I know he needs to be in Berk's. She loves him so much."

"Do you?" Phoebe asked.

"Love him?" Audi sought clarification, and then she continued. "I loved the man he used to be, the man I thought he was. This man, this coward, this so-called husband, can fuck off."

Phoebe stood there, almost in awe. Audi Pence had changed. Either life's hardships had inevitably hardened her, or the stress of her daughter's sudden illness had completely clouded her mind, and she was saying things she truly did not mean.

The One You're Waiting On

~

When Ben returned with a cup of coffee, Phoebe told Audi she was going to leave. She made Audi promise her to call with any news, even it was in the middle of the night. They hugged again, but this time Audi didn't feel as if their connection was the same. Phoebe's words earlier had stung. She wasn't the sympathetic friend Audi had known and loved. It was almost as if she was on Ben's side, and had condoned his cheating. Audi brushed off those questions in her mind, and told her to be safe driving back to St. Louis.

Audi walked over to the window again. She was desperately worried about Berkley and what those technicians were seeing on that MRI right now. She wished she could have gone along with her, to hold her hand. She continued to stare out of the window, a blank stare where she wasn't focused on anything at all. She just didn't want to face Ben in the same room again. But she knew she had to, eventually. At the moment though, it wasn't necessary because she heard the door close and noticed he had walked out again.

~

In the parking lot, Wes was getting out of his car. He had already closed and locked the doors with his key remote when he realized he left his cell phone on the front passenger seat. He unlocked his car again, and got back inside. As he retrieved his phone and was sitting behind the steering wheel, he noticed a woman with long, dark hair walking to her car…and a man wearing a suit, sans a tie, followed quickly on her heels. She turned when he called her name. They stopped between two cars, and embraced. And then Wes watched them kiss with a little too much passion and intensity in a parking lot in broad daylight.

Chapter 15

Audi left the empty hospital room to pace the long hallway. She wished she would have been adamant about staying with Berkley, but she had been so willing to go alone with the nurse that Audi didn't want to change her mind, or make her feel more nervous than she already was at times in that hospital setting.

What was happening in there right now? Was the MRI machine detecting more cancer? Please God, no. What my little girl was going through was already enough. More than any child should have to endure.

Almost the entire length of the hallway from where she was standing, Audi could see the huge elephant that Berkley and Phoebe selected from the hospital's gift shop. Behind it, she saw the legs of a nurse. It looked comical, and Audi smiled as she walked down the hallway to meet her.

"She's doing fine," the nurse told Audi as soon as she approached her. "I just thought I'd put this big guy back in her room for when her test is completed."

Audi smiled again at the ridiculous size of that stuffed animal. "How much longer?"

"Less than thirty minutes," the nurse stated. And then she looked like she wanted to say more, but she didn't. She was a mother too, and she could only imagine the fear of that nightmare.

Audi walked the full length of the hallway, up and down, back and forth, twice. And when she was about to do it all over again, the elevator door opened where she stood and she looked right at him. Her eyes went right to that shirt again. *Comfortably Numb*. She smiled. He smiled. And he noticed her staring. "I really do own more than three shirts," he grinned and his eyes looked greener to her. "I just pack light."

Audi happened to be awfully fond of that shirt. She hadn't told him about her Pink Floyd shirt that she slept in. "I'm not complaining," she said, as they stood off to the side of the open elevator. No one else had been on it, but the doors hadn't closed.

"I have yet to hear you truly complain about anything. How are you holding up?" He briefly touched her arm at the elbow.

"I don't know," she sighed. "Berkley is having an MRI right now."

"It's going to be clear," he said, hoping to God it was. "She's going to be okay."

"I wish for that with all I am," she said, leaning into him, and he opened his arms to her. His embrace. Just the feeling of being in his arms, comforted her like nothing else could right now. Time stood still when she was with him.

"Audi..." She heard her name but it was not Wes' voice close to her ear. This came from close by... and it was Ben.

They parted from each other's arms. Audi looked at Ben, and then back at Wes.

"What's going on?" Ben asked her. As if she owed him an explanation.

"Berkley is still having the MRI, and I'm waiting." She completely ignored Ben's glares and expectation of more from her. *Like, who was the man whose arms were around her?*

"And you are?" Ben asked Wes.

"He's a guest at Gran's B&B," Audi spoke before Wes, "and he's been incredibly supportive to me through Gran's health scare and now Berkley's. Wes, this is Ben, Berkley's father." She never called him her husband and that instantly unnerved Ben. *Why should she have? He left. He cheated.* Even so,

Ben stood there feeling as if she was still his. And seeing her so comfortably enveloped in another man's arms affected him.

Neither one offered a hand to the other. Ben only stared at Audi, while Wes stared at him. An expensive dark suit, sans the tie. Dark hair, every short strand gelled perfectly in place. Wes had a photographic memory. He never forgot a face. He knew this was the same cocky man he had just watched in the parking lot. The question was, who had he been with? *And did Audi know for certain her husband who abandoned her and their child was having an affair?* If not, Wes wasn't sure he wanted to be the one to tell her. He did, however, want that son of a bitch out of Audi's life.

"Can we talk? Privately?" Ben asked, again ignoring Wes beside her.

"We already did that," Audi told him, and Wes observed how different she was with him. He could see and feel her negative energy toward him. This man had hurt her terribly.

"It's okay, I'll grab us water or sodas?" Wes suggested. "Coke, okay?" he winked at her, as they both remembered the last time he brought her both a Coke and a water and she chose what she wanted from the rear end pockets of his faded denim.

She suppressed a giggle, as he walked away. With a scowl on his face, Ben walked in front of her and into Berkley's empty hospital room.

"Seriously?" Ben asked her as she closed the door behind her. "Are you and he...?"

"I'm not screwing around on you, Ben, if that's what you're asking." *Sure could have fooled him. Their closeness was insanely obvious.*

"Then why is he here? It's awkward and it will be when he gets back and we are all waiting for Berkley and the results of the MRI."

"Awkward for you, Ben?" Audi asked. "You left. You wanted someone else. Our marriage is all but over, right?"

"I think we should handle one thing at a time. Berkley comes first."

Fuck you. You haven't put her first in months. "My daughter has always come first with me. Can you say the same?"

"I'm here for her," he stated through a clenched jaw.

"Good. She needs you," Audi paused. *But don't think I do. Not anymore.*

"This waiting is nerve wrecking," he sighed, stuffing his hands in the pockets of his dress pants and rocking on his heels.

"Tell me about it," Audi said, squeezing the foot of the stuffed elephant that was taking up most of the bed she stood beside.

There was giggling outside of the door and Audi immediately looked up. "Can we come in?" Berkley's sweet voice asked, from atop one of Wes' shoulders. Audi thought they looked adorable together. She quickly stepped away from the bed and made her way over to them as Wes carefully ducked under the doorway and then lifted Berkley down before he placed her into Audi's arms. She held her extra close. "Were the nurses good to you?"

Berkley nodded her head. "They said that's my last test, but I still have to stay here for surgery."

"And then we will get out of here for a very long time!" Ben chimed in from across the room, but Audi wished he hadn't said that. No one knew that for sure.

~

Just minutes after Berkley was back in her room, Ben stepped out into the hallway. He had his phone to his ear, as he leaned up against a bare wall. Phoebe answered on the second ring.

"What do you know about this Wes guy who's staying at the B&B?"

"So she told you about him?"

"What is there to tell?"

"Apparently they are really attracted to each other," Phoebe said, feeling guilty for breaking Audi's trust, but she already had done so much worse.

"So my wife has a lover?" Phoebe heard the jealousy in his tone. The way he claimed her as his *wife*, made it blatantly obvious how much he still wanted her. That was their initial plan. Neither one of them were going to leave their spouses.

The One You're Waiting On

"As far as I know, they've only kissed," Phoebe told him. "Ben, do you want her back? I've told you it's sex between us, that's all." He closed his eyes for a moment and leaned his head back against the wall. *But what if he couldn't give her up? What if their passion was too intense to ignore?* He loved his wife, but he wasn't in love with her anymore and had not been for a very long time. He could fall for Phoebe. He questioned if he already had. The way she spoke of them as just messing around without having feelings for each other was how he was forcing himself to think – and feel.

"I can't answer that. She hates me now. And we have to focus on Berkley. She has to get well before we make any rash decisions about our marriage. I just wanted to call you, hear your voice," he told her, and she smiled.

"Are you coming back to the house tonight?"

"Yes, as soon as we speak to the doctor."

"I'll see you later then."

Ben smiled and ended the call. He already felt better.

He stayed out of the room. He was going to check at the nurse's desk to see how much longer it would be for them to wait for the doctor. *Any excuse not to go back into that room.* Ben believed Audi was doing that to him on purpose. She had her new *friend* hanging around to punish him.

Berkley started to nod off, and Audi turned off the light above her bed. "Get some rest. I'll be here," she told her, after she kissed her cheek.

Wes met her on the other side of the room, where a curtain had been drawn. There was not another patient sharing that space, so Audi led him over to the window.

"Should I be here?" he asked her, quietly.

"Only if you want to be," she stated.

"I want to be," he told her.

"I'm sick with worry. This wait is killing me."

Wes brushed a blonde curl away from her eye. "I know that," he said. "Lean on me, no matter what."

"Don't say no matter what..." she felt the tears pool in her eyes.

"What I meant was...no matter what life throws at you, I want to be here for you. Here, now, or decades from now."

"We're crazy," she told him, and smiled.

"I'm crazy about you." His hand was under her jawline again. He moved closer. She moved closer. Their lips were inches apart. It was a good thing there was a curtain separating them from being in plain sight because just as their lips were inching closer, the door to Berkley's hospital room opened and in walked Ben with the doctor.

They pulled away from each other and Wes followed Audi. She drew back the curtain and Ben shot her a disapproving look. The doctor spoke. "Mrs. Pence?"

"Call me Audi."

The One You're Waiting On

"Audi, I would like to discuss your daughter's test results." She instantly brought him over to the other side of the room, away from her sleeping daughter. Wes closed the curtain after all of them were over there.

Ben stood next to Audi and the doctor stood across from them. Wes stayed near the doctor as he began to speak. "Your daughter will have to have a nephrectomy. Her right kidney should be removed as soon as possible. Tomorrow morning is the plan for surgery."

"So you know for sure you have to remove it now?" Audi interjected.

"Yes, the mass is too large not to," the doctor explained, and Audi swallowed hard. Before she could ask if the cancer had spread anywhere else, the doctor spoke again. "With the exception of her kidney, Berkley is clear of cancer in her body." Audi felt her knees weaken. This was good news, but even still the relief of it had taken a sudden toll on her. Wes launched quickly toward her and immediately held her up. Ben had been feeling the same sense of relief, but she had not turned to him, nor he to her. He only stood there, watching her find comfort from another man. He told himself that he *deserved this*. But it still sucked anyway.

"Oh dear God! Thank you so much, doctor!"

"I'm happy to report this, believe me," the doctor smiled sincerely.

"Just get rid of the rest, all of it from her kidney," Audi nearly pleaded.

"I will do all I can. I'll send in a nurse with the details of the surgery, which will be first thing in the morning." Audi nodded her head, and grasped the doctor's hand with gratitude when he offered it to her.

When the doctor walked out, Ben spoke. "I'm going home. I will be back in the morning. Will you text me the surgery time when you have it?"

"Yes, I will," was all Audi said to him, all she really had a chance to say, because he was already stepping away from her and gone from the room.

Wes turned her toward him by her shoulders, and looked in her eyes. They were teary, and still very scared for her child, but at the moment she was incredibly relieved. "Good news for your beautiful girl," his voice was all but a whisper.

"Thank God," she sighed. "And thank you for being here. I don't know what else to say."

"You don't have to thank me, and you don't have to say anything," Wes told her.

"You should go, too…" she told him.

"If you tell me to go back to the B&B and write, I'm going to hush your mouth with a kiss. You know, one of those kisses that goes on and on…"

Audi blushed in the dim-lit room. "I might like that…"

Wes laughed, and she smiled wide at him. "What can I do for you? Is there anything you need or want?" he asked.

"I need to tell Gran what's going on, but I don't want to upset and worry her."

"I think, from what you've told me about your Gran, you are underestimating her strength. She can handle this. She would want to know, and be here."

"I'll go to her tomorrow, but I won't leave here until I know my little girl is going to be okay."

Wes pulled her into his arms and kissed her on top of those blonde curls. He already knew what he had to do. And he would do it first thing in the morning.

Chapter 16

Audi cried hard when she had to separate from Berkley. Afterward, when she regained her composure, she was grateful Berkley had been relaxed and already fading to sleep from the anesthetic that was dripping into her IV. She didn't need to see – and remember – her mommy falling apart. Ben's eyes were red as he walked away. He knew he shouldn't try to comfort his wife. He and Audi had hardly said more than a few words to each other. Their focus was on their daughter. They were alone with Berkley prior to the surgery, but Wes would soon be there. He purposely stayed away all morning, and Audi believed she understood why. She and Ben were Berkley's parents. They needed time alone with her. But that wasn't the main reason why Wes arrived at the hospital late. He had Nurse Jo with him so Gran would feel more comfortable when he picked her up at The Villa and drove her to Anderson Hospital. Nurse Jo also had been the one to tell Gran about Berkley. Wes knew Audi wanted to, but time was of the essence – and Wes chose to bring Audi who she needed most right now.

The One You're Waiting On

Audi had gone outside. She couldn't stand the four walls of that waiting room, or being alone in there with Ben. She had thought Phoebe would have been there. When Phoebe called her early this morning with good wishes, she only said she would be there in spirit but never gave a reason why she wasn't coming.

The warm wind picked up as Audi sat down on a bench outside of the hospital, near a sidewalk. Wes, Nurse Jo, and Gran saw her, but Audi didn't notice them. Gran told the two of them to allow her to walk over there alone.

When Audi looked up, the surprise on her face quickly turned into a broken sob. Gran held her after she stood up and ran to her. This woman wasn't fragile. She was a pillar of strength, and Audi was quickly reminded of that now. While wiping her tears, Audi helped Gran over to the bench. She was still a little slow to move, but already much stronger.

"You came," Audi smiled.

"Absolutely, as soon as I heard."

"Wes?" Audi asked, implying it was him who brought her there. *That's where he had been. My goodness, that man, and how he knew exactly what she needed.*

"And his sidekick, Nurse Jo," Gran admitted.

Audi smiled with teary eyes. "God love them for knowing I needed you here."

"I'm so sorry, Audi girl," Gran paused. The last thing she would ever want to be alive for was to witness her Audi feel the pain of losing a child, as she had.

"She has to be okay, Gran. Has to be."

"The doctor told you he could get it all, right? No treatments, just removal of her kidney, correct?"

"That's what he said," Audi choked on a sob. She was more emotional now, not being around Berkley, and having Gran there. "But things can go wrong, or change. Cancer can come back with a vengeance. I don't want this for my little girl."

"Who the hell does!" Gran was always quick to bring her back to reality. "You can't choose the poor me path, Audi girl. You take this. Sure, it sucks and it's unfair, but you look for your blessings. Berkley is going to be okay. You still have her here, minus one organ." Audi knew where Gran was coming from with her hostile attitude and strong faith. What a combination. When Audi lost her mother, Gran lost her daughter. That gentle, special woman was one in the same. And both Audi and Gran missed her to no end. Gran's hostility lessened a little with time, and her faith grew stronger. Audi wondered if Gran's recent health issues had her thinking her time to be with her loved ones in heaven was getting closer. Audi didn't want to ask her because one of her greatest fears was to lose Gran. Yes, Grandpa Art and their daughter were waiting. But not yet. Gran was still needed here.

"I know, I hear what you're saying but so much has changed in my life in just a couple of months. My husband left. Your heart issues are scaring me beyond words. If you die on me, Berkley is all I have left."

"No one is dying on you. And what did I just tell you? Look for your blessings. Now I know I'm old and all, but I'm not blind. There's a sexy thing from Utah still hanging around, wanting to make you happy."

"You like Wes, don't you?" Audi grinned.

"I like what he does for you. Ben never could be that guy for you in eight or nine years, but this man has already worked magic in just days."

"He has, Gran," Audi agreed. "What am I going to do about that?"

"Don't let him get away."

Audi smiled, and squeezed Gran's hand. "I'll try not to."

~

This was the longest wait of Audi's life. Nothing, no matter how bad in her life, had ever compared to this for her. She was beyond terrified. She tried not to imagine what was happening to her little girl's tiny body in that operating room. The doctor had told them he would first attempt to remove the kidney through laparoscopic surgery. That involved the use of a wand-like camera that passed through a series of small incisions in the abdominal wall, and was used to view the abdominal cavity and remove the kidney through only a small incision. Audi prayed, over and over, for that particular procedure to be successful for Berkley. Otherwise, the surgeon would have to make an incision in her abdomen, possibly even temporarily remove a rib to take out her kidney that particular way. Audi was overthinking and she needed to stop. An hour and a half had gone by, and she had at least that much longer to wait until it was over.

They were all in the same waiting area – Gran, Nurse Jo, Wes, Audi, and Ben. Ben, to be polite, had said hello to Gran when he first saw her, and after glaring at him long enough to see him squirm in his chair, Gran spoke his name with no expression on her face, *Ben…*

Ben had no doubt Gran was a force to be reckoned with. And he wasn't thrilled to see her there. He was certain she felt the same way about seeing him. They all just needed to keep in mind why they were gathered there. *For Berkley.*

As time passed, however, nerves wore thin, and it was Ben who lost his composure first. Nurse Jo had taken Gran for a short walk down the hallway to stretch her legs, and stop in the cafeteria for something to eat. Gran still tired out quickly, and Audi already told her she didn't have to stay at the hospital for the duration of the surgery. She would call her later at The Villas with any news. While Audi was concerned about Gran, Wes' focus was on her. And that was what annoyed Ben to no end. *How many times did he ask her if she needed anything? How often did he touch her hand, resting on her lap while she was lost in thought? Or prayer. Or agony.*

"I know you're consumed with worry," Ben heard Wes quietly say to Audi as he watched her turn to him. They way she looked at him sent Ben reeling inside. *She used to look at him the same way, didn't she?* He watched another man move a curl from her eye, that one blonde spiral hair that was always defiant. "You still need to take care of yourself. Eat something. I'll get it for you, or walk with you."

"I don't think I can stomach anything yet…not until I know Berkley is out of surgery." Audi reached into her handbag and retrieved a Chapstick and she moisturized her lips while she spoke.

"Berkley needs you well, and strong," Wes started to say, and Ben finally interjected. He couldn't take it anymore. He lost his self-control.

"For Chrissakes, man! She's a grown woman, more than capable of taking care of herself!" Ben spat those words, completely uncaring about his outburst.

"Ben, please," Audi spoke, trying to sound calm, but there was an obvious scowl on her face. And Wes thought it would be best to ignore him.

"What? It's inappropriate for him to be here! Berkley is *our* daughter."

"I see your point," Wes spoke up. "And I will leave, if Audi asks me to." Audi wanted to smile. Wes knew she wouldn't ask him to leave.

Ben scoffed. "You are still my wife," he said to Audi.

"Oh? Could have fooled me. Last I heard from you, weeks ago, you needed time. After so many ignored messages, I began to feel not just abandoned – but angry. I've tried, really tried, to set that anger aside for Berkley. We need to get her through this, together. And, when she's well, I want you to make up for lost time with her. Be her father. As for me, don't ever call me your wife again."

Wes was looking down at the floor at his feet. He did feel like a third wheel at this point in their conversation, but he was in awe of Audi. When he met her, she was a woman hurting and possibly pining for her runaway husband. Now, her strength and independence was commendable. And Ben deserved every bit of her wrath.

Ben wanted to get up and storm out of there, but he didn't. Because if he did, Wes would win. And he wasn't about to let another man win.

Footsteps approached the waiting area outside, and someone turned the handle on the door to enter. They were given a private waiting area, so Audi knew it was either Gran and Nurse Jo coming back already, or an update from the medical staff. She tensed as she watched the door.

Her long dark hair was pulled back into a low ponytail, and she wore a scoopneck powder blue sundress and heeled sandals. Not quite the attire for a hospital waiting room, but that was Phoebe. Always dressed fit to kill.

Ben's eyes widened. *He thought they agreed it was best for her to stay away.*

Wes creased his brow. *Who was that woman? He remembered her from somewhere.*

And Audi was instantly on her feet. "You came!" They embraced. Ben watched them, but forced his eyes away. And Wes was watching Ben. He squirmed on his chair just as he had when Gran walked in. To say he was uncomfortable would be an understatement.

"I couldn't stay away," Audi heard Phoebe say in her ear before they parted from their close embrace. And Audi wondered why Phoebe felt she had to stay away.

"Thank you. You know what your presence always does for me." Phoebe reached for Audi's hand as she glanced at Ben… and then over at Wes. Audi saw this, and spoke first. "Phoebe, this is Wes Delahunt, the famous author I was telling you about."

Famous author? Ben frowned. That was new information for him.

Phoebe took a few steps toward where Wes was seated, and he politely stood up and offered his hand. "Very nice to meet you."

"Phoebe is my neighbor, back in St. Louis, and my dearest friend in the world," Audi offered, and Wes watched Phoebe tilt her head and smile. That movement, that gesture, jogged his memory. He knew where he had seen her before. *Holy Shit.*

Wes glanced from Phoebe over to Ben. He was looking down at his feet on the floor, and was clearly uncomfortable. *Those two people in Audi's world had betrayed her in the worst way, and were continuing to deceive her.*

Wes needed to get Audi alone. He had to confide in her about what he saw. She deserved to know the truth. No matter how devastating it was.

Chapter 17

Although they weren't sitting near each other, nor speaking, Wes observed the body language between Audi's husband and her best friend. It's what he did, but he always tried to do so nonchalantly. He studied people. Their mannerisms. Their personalities. Their interactions. This seemed too unreal to be true. But, he was certain. He knew what he saw in the hospital parking lot.

The One You're Waiting On

Another forty-five minutes had passed, and by then both Gran and Nurse Jo were back in the waiting room. They all, sans Ben, shared small talk to pass the time. It was when a nurse, wearing aqua-colored scrubs, peeked through the door, that the room fell silent. Audi was the one she spoke directly to. She was the one who had camped out at the hospital beside her daughter for two days, never having left her since she brought her into the ER for a fall. Who knew that fall from a swing could lead to something so serious? Audi would forever remember that ER doctor's words, *this was a blessing in disguise.* Maybe so. If – being on that swing, and then falling from it – had saved Berkley's life.

Audi was already on her feet in the middle of the room. Everyone else remained seated, as the nurse spoke. "Dr. Barnes wanted me to tell you that your little girl did just fine. She'll be in recovery within the next fifteen or twenty minutes. I will come back to get you when you can see her." Audi glanced at Ben across the room, and then back at the nurse. *Thank you so much.*

~

Two weeks later...

She did it. She never thought she would be able to look at that swingset at the B&B again, much less go near it. But Audi was sitting on the swing that changed everything for Berkley. Sometimes she wanted to curse the doctor who called Berkley's accident a blessing in disguise. Cancer was cancer. No matter how much or how little, that shit was terrifying. Other times she tried so hard to force herself to count her blessings like Gran reminded her to do. But lately, she had failed at it.

She gripped both of the rusty chains on that old swing and raised her feet off the ground. She was at the swing's mercy. She wasn't gliding high, as the warm wind was blowing wildly through her blonde curls. She closed her eyes and imagined free-falling. Yes, free-falling. From a high place. With nothing to hold onto. Not a thing to brace her fall. That's how her life felt. And Audi wasn't sure how to stop. And regain control.

Gran had been living back at the B&B for two days. She was doing well, and physically felt better than she had in a very long time. She welcomed the idea of Nurse Jo running the B&B with her and Audi, especially since she arrived home and half of the six rooms were booked.

And just now, Gran made her way through the grass and joined Audi on the swingset. She had a harder time squeezing her rear end onto the swing than she had in years past, but she managed as she gripped the chains and plopped down, not so gracefully. Audi had stopped her own swing in place to watch Gran wiggle her way between the chains and onto the bendy rubber.

She knew Gran was checking up on her out there. "I don't know how much longer I can do this," Audi sighed, and Gran understood.

"So where will you go? Back to your home in St. Louis?"

"It's not much of a home anymore." A For Sale sign was on display in the front yard, while Ben was living there. Her most recent trip to that house, a house they used to call *theirs*, would forever be frozen in her mind as a bad memory.

~

One week ago...

As Audi drove into the Tower Grove South subdivision, it felt familiar yet different to be back there again. She glanced at Phoebe's massive colonial-style home on her right, before making a left onto her own driveway directly across the street. For almost seven years, that beautiful home served as a safe harbor. It was difficult to gaze up at it now as she ascended the slanted driveway on foot, toward the front door. She had the house key in her hand. She assumed Ben was at work, as it was still ninety minutes before quitting time. And she hoped to be gone from the house by the time he did arrive.

The turn of her key released the lock. The foyer was well lit with natural light from the sun peering through the large front windows in that house. *My, how she once loved everything about that old colonial house.* A part of her wanted to walk slowly through every room, open every closet and drawer. The other side of her mentality just wanted to hightail it up the stairway and into the last room on the right, and make her way straight into the walk-in closet and get the black dress she came for.

She wouldn't go into Berkley's room. She couldn't. *Why was she doing this to herself? She could have purchased another black* dress. *Did she even care what she would wear on the worst day of her life? What the hell did it matter?* Her thoughts raced as she felt heartless, standing at the base of the stairs. And then a noise jolted her into focus.

The sound came from upstairs. As if something was knocking against a wall. Audi started up the stairs. If Ben was home, he must have parked in the garage and closed the door.

When Audi reached the second level, she realized what she heard. She cringed at the thought. The headboard. On their bed. Sometimes it would bump up against the wall. It wasn't a surprise that Ben was cheating on her. He admitted it. *But to hear it? See it? Witness it?*

She forced herself to put one foot in front of the other. She heard a woman cry out. Not in pain. In pleasure. Audi thought she was going to be sick to her stomach.

The door to *their bedroom* was partly open. *Their bedding* was disheveled and stripped down to only a midnight blue fitted and flat sheet. The matching duvet and decorative pillows were scattered across the hardwood floor. Along with clothes and underwear.

Wes had tried to tell her, but Audi wasn't convinced. *He was new to the area. He didn't know people. Every face was one of a stranger. There was absolutely no way her best friend would ever betray her.* Wes reluctantly dropped his case, and Audi remembered being miffed at him for the very first time. Other disagreements between them would follow.

But now she saw her dark hair, down and tousled. The forced contact between the headboard and the wall had ceased.

She watched her nude husband flat on his back, and her every bit as naked best friend riding him. And with his release, he groaned her name. Another woman's name. *Phoebs!* Audi then stared at how Phoebe bent her body forward and Ben sat upright to meet her halfway. They kissed like they were filming for an x-rated movie.

Audi shoved the partially open door so hard against the wall that it bent the stopper and the force of the doorknob punctured a hole in the wall. Their naked bodies reacted in surprise and immediately pulled away from each other. Audi heard Phoebe scream and Ben spewed a few curse words.

"I would have never believed this...had I not seen it. You? Phoebe? My best friend. Did I ever really know you?" Audi stared as she spoke to her. The fact that they were both completely exposed humiliated them. They were never supposed to get caught.

Phoebe covered herself with the loose bed sheet. Ben didn't bother. Phoebe had a look of pure horror on her face. Audi nearly smirked at her as she passed the foot end of the bed and made her way over to the closet. She opened the door, quickly found her modest black dress with the ruffle hem. She also reached for her black heels. By now, Ben was standing up beside their bed, pulling on his black suit pants, sans any underwear. Phoebe was still frozen in place on Audi's side of the bed.

"You bitch..." Audi spoke in an eerily calm voice. And then she moved her glaring eyes from her best friend to her husband. "And you," Ben stared back with remorse in his eyes.

But Audi didn't want to recognize any of it. "You make me sick. Just when I thought my life couldn't crumble anymore...you take more from me." Audi was partly referring to her now no-longer best friend.

"Audi, we are all hurting..." Ben attempted to explain.

"No! Stop. You stop right there. Do not blame our loss on this!" Audi stretched out her arms in front of her and gestured with both of her hands toward their bed. "It's been her all along, hasn't it?" Audi saw the guilt on Phoebe's face, and she watched Ben nod his head. *Wes was right. Of course he was.*

Audi had nothing left to say. She started to leave their bedroom at a much quicker pace than when she first entered.

Neither one of them called after her. *Not that she wanted them to.* And when she reached the open doorway, she turned back around. Her black dress was draped over her right forearm, and her black heels hung from her fingertips.

"I would have found out eventually," she assured them. *They were both liars and cheats who deserved each other.* "I don't care what you two do with your lives. It's no concern to me anymore. You're both dead to me..." The tears were beginning to fiercely pool in her eyes. Eyes that were now focused solely on Ben. "Just like our little girl."

~

The One You're Waiting On

Just hours following Berkley's nephrectomy surgery...

Audi was on the heels of the nurse, and Ben was following Audi. They were en route to the surgical recovery room. They were told Berkley was beginning to wake up. Coming off the anesthetic, they expected she would be drowsy and possibly talking out of her head. Audi could not wait to see her, touch her, hold her when her little body didn't hurt to move. It would take her some time to heal. She prayed Berkley would not be in too severe of pain. Audi was going to do everything she could to help her little girl recover safely. Knowing she would only have one kidney now made Audi want to place her child in a bubble. To protect her from any harm. That was going to be near impossible, she knew, and she smiled at the thought of her adventurous daughter.

Just as the nurse started to push open the recovery room door, they all heard the commotion. *Get the doctor STAT!* Two nurses were screaming and scurrying in pure panic mode. Audi pushed past the nurse in front of her and Ben, and that's when she saw blood. On the floor. On the bed. On a lifeless Berkley. The scene was horrific, and Audi's adrenaline kicked in something fierce as she pushed the nurse out of her way. Ben stayed back. He was shocked into numbness. *Get her out of here!* The doctor screamed as he only saw Audi when he flew into the room. Ben was slouching in the corner, with wide eyes and an open mouth.

Everyone sprung into action. Audi refused to leave, and the medical staff immediately stopped trying to force her away. They chose to focus on saving this little person's life.

Audi heard something about the *blood being unable to clot Getting her into surgery to stop the internal bleeding.* Time froze. Time flew. Audi had no idea which. She stood there, feeling helpless. She spoke out in loud screams, *Berkley don't die! Don't die baby girl! God, oh God, please, please, save her...*

The bed was dripping with blood as it spun on its wheels past Audi. She threw herself in the way of it, and pressed her face against Berkley's. Audi's mouth was close to Berkley's little ear. Her face was deathly pale. Her eyes were closed. There was blood trickling from her airways. "Come back to me," Audi spoke in choked sobs as someone wasted no time and jerked her off of her child as the gurney sped off in a dire state of emergency.

It was Ben who had forced her to back off. He had snapped out of his trance. He cried when he spoke to his wife, *let them take her or she's going to die.* Audi abruptly pulled away from him, out of his arms. She didn't need his comfort. And she certainly wouldn't listen to how their daughter might die.

The emergent commotion down the hallway had caught the attention of Wes, Gran, Nurse Jo, and Phoebe. They were standing outside of the recovery room door when the medical staff surrounding Berkley's gurney rushed out and past them. The scene was horrific. Nurse Jo immediately tended to Gran, worried her heart would not be able to take this. She herself could not take it. Phoebe was silent, and stared at both Ben and Audi through the open door. Audi's hands and clothes were covered in blood, as was Ben from touching her, forcing her to move back. It was Wes who stepped into that doorway first. Audi saw him and fell to her knees in sobs. Wes was right there, he met his denim clad knees with the bloody floor to hold her up. "Blood...her blood was not clotting properly... she's hemorrhaging..." Audi's words were sporadic, but through her sobs, Wes understood. And he had never been more scared in his life. It terrified him to think what would happen to this woman if she lost her child.

∼

The time between being told her little girl was in recovery to the moment Dr. Barnes returned from the operating room for the second time, covered in blood, with tears rolling down his cheeks, was a complete blur. *How did this happen?* Audi was *inconsolable. Wes tried. Gran tried. Ben intervened.* And finally, the medical staff at Anderson Hospital felt as if they had no other choice. Audi was constrained and injected with a sedative. It was a heartbreaking scene. There wasn't a dry eye in the room.

As she lay too still in a bed, where Wes was the only one left in a room with her, he sat close and held her hand, blotched with dried blood. Even if Audi was too drugged to know he was there, Wes wanted to be close to her.

Hours had passed before he stepped out of the room briefly to make a phone call in the hallway. He called his publisher. After Wes told him the utterly awful story, his exact words to a man he worked with and considered a friend were, "Dan, I don't care if I ever write again. I'll just live off the profit from my previous books, or I may be forced to get a real job. I just want her. I'm in love with a woman who just lost her everything. I have to pull her through."

Gran was uncomfortable with the silence between them on the swings. There was too much of it lately. Audi was withdrawn from everything and everyone. Yes, Gran had seen her like this before, when she was a child and left parentless. This time, however, was different. Even more awful. And only Gran understood. Losing a child was something she too never had gotten over. And never would. But she had to convince Audi to put one foot in front of the other and survive.

"Your pain right now is inconceivable," Gran began. "You've lost too much in such little time."

"I don't care about Ben or Phoebe," Audi spoke, staring straight ahead as she lifted her feet up off the ground and the swing moved, forward and then back.

"Of course you don't. They don't matter in comparison to sweet Berkley." Just the mention of her name, her memory, sprung tears to Audi's eyes. There was never a pain like this for her. Not even the day she lost her own mother. "Get rid of your husband. Divorce him. Sell your house. Never go back to those memories. Leave your best friend in the dust with him. Sure, it hurts to be betrayed, but be the better person and overcome what they did to you." Audi stopped her swing again to listen to Gran. She never turned her head to look at her though. "Carry your memories of your baby girl close to your heart. Relive those times, and those feelings. But, honey, do not let it consume you. Find something for you. Something that will allow your heart to heal, and you to move on with your life. If you cannot stay here, go." Gran was the most selfless person Audi had ever known. Gran recognized Audi's strength all of her life, and she would stop at nothing now to help her see it and use it to power through the unbearable pain.

"Other than you, and this place, I have nothing left." Audi stated.

"That's not true," Gran begged to differ. "You pushed him away. He didn't want to leave here, or you. He's the kind of man who will wait forever, you know."

Audi shook her head. "Why? Why would he want to saddle his life with someone who feels like I do? I'm barely hanging on, Gran. Wes deserves better."

~

Two days after Berkley's memorial service...

"Just go," Audi had told Wes. Physically pushing him away and rejecting any comfort he offered her had not convinced him that she was done. She was in so much pain, shocked and consumed with grief. "Go back home, to Utah, to your family, your career."

"I'm not leaving you. You know how I feel."

"Yes, you love me," Audi said in a cynical tone. "Well I cannot return those feelings to you. I don't have it in me to love anyone anymore. It's not worth the pain. I've told you that. We've been over this too many times. Just fucking leave me alone."

Wes tried everything possible. He talked. He attempted to hold her and not say anything at all. He begged Audi not to shut him out. He even lost his patience and raised his voice, trying his hand at tough love. He confessed his feelings, bared his heart and soul. He had never fought harder for anything or anyone in his entire life.

But eventually, he left the B&B.

Chapter 18

In Cove Fort, Utah, Wes returned to his old, refurbished farm house on more than one hundred acres of land. It was his home, and he'd always welcomed the solace he found alone out there. But, upon his return to Utah, he had felt anything but comfort and peace. After two and a half weeks in Illinois, he had returned heartbroken. The loss of that child did him in. *God should have saved her.* None of what happened was fair, and Audi had been completely destroyed. It saddened him to no end to know her spirit had died with her child.

Since he had returned home, Wes had not slept and only consumed coffee and Coke to keep him going. He had finished writing his book. He wanted to tell Audi. She was the first person he thought of. She, and the B&B, had inspired him to take his story in a different direction. It was complete and he had just emailed it to his publisher. He hoped, in a few months, to see it released and well-received. But, the book was not what he was thinking about now, as he sat on his old front porch, looking out at the long, narrow lane road that stirred up dust anytime anyone drove on it. And right now he saw an old beat up pickup truck, one that resembled the Walton's family vehicle on the 1970s television show. His big sister, Robyn, had always said she wanted to own a truck just like that one. One that wouldn't always be reliable, but had a classic, old, antique look. He smiled at the sight of her behind the wheel in it. She often had her twin two-year-olds fussing side-by-side in car seats next to her, but not this time. She was alone. As much as Wes adored his nephews, he was relieved to see just Robyn.

"Hey little brother," Robyn said, slamming the door to her old truck. It didn't quite catch, so she reopened it and slammed it harder, forcing it to seal that time. She nearly reached Wes' six-foot height, topping off just two inches shorter than him. Her long sandy brown hair was poker straight, where his was naturally curly, especially when it was overgrown.

"Hey yourself," Wes said, standing up from his old wooden rocking chair on the porch. She wore dark brown gladiator sandals, cut-off jean shorts, and a white v-neck t-shirt which instantly reminded him of Audi.

When she reached the porch, Wes opened his arms to her. She squeezed him in a hug that only a sister could give.

They were just fourteen months apart in age, but the comfort she brought to him had always felt motherly and wise.

"You okay?" she asked him. "Mom filled me in on everything." Wes had called his mother on his long drive home. They had talked for hours. And it was the first time since he was a boy that he broke down and cried.

"Not really," he admitted. "She was in so much pain, Rob. It sucked. I tried so hard to reach her, but I only pushed her farther away."

"It's too much for her, Wesley." His sister was the only person who called him Wesley. He always felt boyish when she did. "Her emotions are entirely too raw right now. She needs time. And a lot of it."

"So you're saying I shouldn't give up on her?" Wes needed to hear someone else tell him that. He had no intention of letting Audi slip through his fingers, but hearing his sister tell him to not to give up would make all the difference in the world to him.

"I hear you love her?" Robyn asked him, with a sweet smile on her face. Despite the tragic circumstances, she was keyed up to know her brother had finally fallen in love for real.

"More than I ever thought possible," he smiled. "She's amazing. She's beautiful, smart, spunky, sexy, and just everything I had no idea I've been waiting on."

Robyn returned an all-teeth, genuine smile to her brother. "Holy shit, you've got it bad, bro."

"And it's tearing me apart inside knowing I'm here and she's there – only because she wanted me to leave."

"She didn't want you to leave."

"Like hell she didn't. She was adamant. She was so closed off and angry."

"She's not angry with you. She pissed at the unfairness that slammed into her life like a freight train. She's shutting down, and even lashing out, because she's hurting. She doesn't know how else to deal. Wes, you know I understand. No one can imagine the pain and heartbreak from losing a child. Unless you've been there."

Robyn saw tears pooling in her brother's eyes. "She was the most beautiful little girl. She had her mama's blonde curls and bright blue eyes. A little sassy, and a lot sweet. God, Rob, I think I fell for her too." The tears freefell from his face. He hadn't shaved in days, and Robyn put both of her hands on his scruff and wiped away his tears that soaked it.

She held him and cried with him. The unfairness of life sucked beyond words sometimes.

~

Audi was lying on the pullout couch bed in the den. The blinds were closed in the middle of the day. She hadn't slept, showered, or eaten. In the bed with her were Berkley's pajamas. She always folded them up and placed them on top of her pillow every morning when she got dressed. Audi was holding the little pink tank top with a daisy stitched on the chest close to her face. *How long before the sweet scent of her little girl would fade from her clothes?* It was thoughts like that which came to her mind, day and night, and always sent her down deeper into her grief.

The door to her makeshift bedroom opened swiftly and Audi never bothered to cover her body. To bed she always wore her favorite Pink Floyd t-shirt and panties.

Gran left the door open and made her way over to the window to open the blinds. "Audi girl, it's two o'clock in the afternoon. Get moving or you'll get too swallowed up in your pain."

"I have no reason to get moving. Berkley was my reason for everything –for living– and she's gone." Audi was still holding tight to the little pajama top.

"Yes, she's gone. And it's fucking unfair." Gran's language never surprised Audi, but her statement did catch her attention. "When my Monica died, I had you to keep me going. Oh I wanted to curl up, give up, and just lose myself...but what would have happened to you?"

"We fought pretty hard to move on, didn't we?" Audi noted. "I've looked back and thought time and again how I had a rough childhood and the pain of that loss never left me. But I made it. I survived. I had you and Gramps. Then I became an adult and met Ben and we had Berkley. Even when he left, I knew eventually I was going to be okay. Because of Berkley. So now what? What's left for me? Not a fucking thing!"

"I agree," Gran stated, standing at the foot end of the couch bed. "You're not yet thirty years old. Give up now and you'll have a good sixty years ahead of you to be bitter and miserable. I'll be long gone so I won't have to watch it!"

Audi kept silent as Gran continued. She had caught her attention this time. "Just promise me you will always remember one thing when you wallow day after day, year after year. Think of what your mother would have given to live a long life. She would not have wasted it, that's for sure." Audi thought of her mother and what she had learned from her in only twelve years. She always looked for the positive – even in the worst situations. And her married life, as an abuse victim, was damn close to the worst. "Audi girl, our faithful and loving God is once again on my shit list. I'm so angry at him right now. First Monica, and now Berkley. I swear when I die the first thing I will do once I barrel through those pearly gates is I will find out the reason why. Why were those two taken from us? And then I'll be back to tell you, so you will not have to live wondering any longer." Audi smiled slightly through more tears. All she did anymore was cry. "I hurt for you. I don't know what to do to pull you up. And I know why I feel so helpless. You think I'm strong. You think I'm wise. You think I can blow past grief and pain like no one else – because I've done it before. Well honey I'm here to tell you that it's a facade. I still cry in the shower. I still shake my finger at the heavens when I'm standing at the graveside of my child who should not have gone before me. I cannot help you. I cannot pick you up and dust off your ass. I'm too old and too tired for this bullshit that's been handed to us again. Let's just get in the car and drive the fucker off of a cliff."

Audi's eyes widened. "Gran..." she spoke in what was barely a whisper. It's not as if she hadn't already gone there in her own mind. "Please stop. It wouldn't take much to talk me into that right now."

"Completely understandable," Gran stated.

"But?" Audi asked her, knowing there was more. With Gran, there was always more.

"But one day you may see there was a plan for you. Just don't close yourself off to your options. Live the life you were meant to live."

"Without my little girl? I was meant to be her mommy. I was robbed of raising her!" Audi choked on a sob, but forced back the tears in her eyes. She was so sick and tired of either crying or feeling like she was about to cry.

"Yes you certainly were," Gran agreed. "Just stay focused. Breathe. Keep your heart open."

Chapter 19

Audi showered, got dressed in jeans and another v-neck t-shirt. Her feet were bare, and her toenails could have used a touch-up with pink polish. That was something she and Berkley did regularly together. They *painted*, as Berkley used to say, each other's toe nails. She used a blow dryer on her wet hair and just left the curls down and untamed when she was finished.

When Audi walked out of her private hallway, she saw Gran seated at the check-in desk, and a couple was just handing over their key and leaving. Audi had no idea who had been staying with them. For days she had only gone from being cooped up in her room to sitting outside on the swing. It was uncanny, but she found some peace on that swing, it was almost as if she felt closer to Berkley there.

When the door closed, Gran heard Audi walk up behind her. "Nice people," Gran commented. "They were our last, so we're vacant again."

Audi knew that meant there were three rooms with adjoining bathrooms upstairs that needed to be cleaned and prepared for more guests. She hadn't been very useful to Gran and Nurse Jo in weeks. She knew Gran was handling the lighter work, but it wasn't fair to Nurse Jo to have to do all of the cleaning and laundry. Nurse Jo was a workhorse, Audi knew that, but she was also thirty-five years older than her.

"I can help Nurse Jo turn those rooms around," Audi offered, and Gran tried to hold back a smile. *Atta girl.*

"She would appreciate that. She'll say it's not necessary though." Gran did smile now.

"I'll go," Audi said, turning around to head up the stairway.

She found Nurse Jo in the second room on the right. Audi tried not to think about Wes when she passed the room he stayed in.

Nurse Jo was on her hands and knees scrubbing the tile floor in the bathroom. It reeked of a strong cleaning chemical in there and as soon as Audi recognized that, she flipped the switch for the vent and then backed out of the bathroom to open a window in the bedroom. "You need some ventilation in here," Audi spoke from the next room, and when Nurse Jo stood up and peeked her head through the doorway, Audi immediately noticed her usual spiked hair was flattened in places, and her overly applied makeup was smeared under her eyes.

"Thank you, honey, it's warm in here too." Audi stepped closer and then she realized it wasn't sweat that was causing Nurse Jo's makeup to run. It was tears.

"You okay?" Audi asked. But she already knew the answer. *What a stupid question. None of them were all right.*

"Fine. Just fine. Keeping busy here, that's for sure."

"I can help," Audi told her.

"When you're ready. No rush. Your Gran is able to do a little more each day around here. I'm grateful for this job, because you know I'm really not needed as Besa's nurse anymore."

"You'll always have a place here," Audi told her, and meant it. And then she thought of her as Berkley's sitter. The games they played. The fun they had together. How selfish had she been, Audi scolded herself. Nurse Jo was being strong for them, but she too was grieving. Hence, her tears when she thought she was alone.

"Thank you," Nurse Jo spoke, and tried to force a stoic expression, but failed when her face flushed and her eyes watered. She looked away, down at the floor. Anywhere but directly at Audi.

Audi stepped closer to her, close enough to reach for her hand, the one she did not have a yellow rubber glove on, and she held it. "I know you miss her. Berkley loved you so very much." *Had Audi ever properly thanked her for all the times in recent months when she entertained Berkley? All those times she brought a smile to her little face, and more often than not, the laughter followed.*

Nurse Jo shook her head, side to side repeatedly, as if to shake away the tears fighting behind her eyes. "Oh my," she spoke, with a hoarse voice, "not half as much as I miss and love her." Audi swallowed hard. And Nurse Jo turned her back to her. Her shoulders began to shake, and Audi grabbed her hard around them.

"You're grieving too. Forgive me for not seeing that, until now." Audi held her tighter.

"Nothing to forgive, honey. You are her mother. Take as long as you need to meet your own needs. To hell with everyone else. You *are* her mother, not *were*. Are! And you always will be."

Audi could have cried, but this time she didn't because she felt a little bit stronger.

~

After the rooms were ready, Gran had lunch prepared for all of them. It was the first time Audi had eaten anything substantial in days. She wondered if Gran prepared her favorite homemade chicken salad wraps for that reason.

Audi made herself useful in the kitchen after they ate, when she cleared their dishes from the table. They had shared comfortable conversation during lunch, with no mention of losing Berkley. Already, Audi sometimes needed that break.

When Gran and Nurse Jo settled into the sitting room, both with the intention of taking a nap, Audi stepped outside again.

The July air was hot and humid, and her jeans suddenly felt as if they were sticking to her legs. Her curly hair would frizz in no time. She made her way directly over to the swing. She always chose the one Berkley had favored.

She sat down, let go of the chains, and pulled her cell phone out of her front pocket and placed it on her lap. Wes had been on her mind again. She was so cruel to him, but Audi felt as if she had no other choice. He would one day regret his decision and resent her if she continued a relationship with him during this saddest, most needy and lonely time for her. Wes deserved better. And she certainly didn't want him to be with her out of pity.

She clicked the Google icon on the home screen. *Wes Delahunt*. She said she would do an online search of him, but never had.

His photograph came up. That face. Those green eyes, and overgrown sandy brown hair. Audi smiled. That's what he did for her. He brought her joy even when she was at the absolute saddest, most devastating time in her life.

Wes Delahunt.com. Beloved storyteller. Three published books. Delahunt knows how to create characters that instantly become a part of your life as you read. You want to know them, befriend them. In every novel that Delahunt pens, you'll find a strong hardworking male character who knows how to take care of his own.

Audi scrolled down farther. Born and raised in Cove Fort, Utah. If she searched deeper, maybe to a website that was not officially his, she would probably find the story about his father. The media often played off of other people's pain. Wes had made no secret of his past, of his father being a drug addict who abandoned his wife and children, and later ended up in prison.

Personal life. Single. Never married. There were several pictures of Wes with different women by his side, or on his arm. That was to be expected, Audi realized, but still she felt a few pangs of jealousy. *Damn, he was so good to her. And for her.* Online, she read that Wes Delahunt would be quite the catch for some lucky woman. After having gotten to know him, and spent so much time with him day after day, Audi knew he wasn't just a catch. He was genuinely a good man, with a heart too big for his own good. He never should have fought so hard for her, because Audi couldn't be the one for him. The more he tried to convince her that they deserved a chance to be together, the harder she resisted. *Let me help you heal. Fall apart and I'll pick up all of the pieces. Let me love you. Let's love each other.* When Wes finally gave in and walked away, Audi believed he had thought he granted her what she wanted. But that could not have been more wrong.

~

That evening, Nurse Jo had gone home as she did at the end of every day. Nine o'clock was their closing time at the B&B. It was five minutes before nine when Audi was in the kitchen, contemplating pouring herself a glass of wine. Then she saw the headlights from a car coming up the drive. She stepped into the living room and waited near the check-in desk.

It took several minutes, once the car was parked and the engine was shut off, before anyone came inside the B&B. When the door opened, Audi saw a young woman, carrying both a diaper bag and a baby. The baby was upright, able to hold its head up, and was maybe three months old or so. Audi stood up, "Hello there. Oh, let me get that door for you." The young woman appeared frazzled or embarrassed, but she did quietly say thank you. Audi closed the front door and grinned at the baby, with only blonde peach fuzz all over her head. A girl, Audi assumed, because she had a pink blanket clutched under her chubby arm. And her ears were already pierced.

"Do you have a room available here?" the young woman asked Audi. "I can't afford much, and the hotels around here are really expensive. For that reason, Audi was relieved Gran never posted her prices. It was ninety-five dollars for one night's stay.

"I understand," Audi said, and she felt sympathetic for her. She recalled Gran warning her of the sob stories given by guests over the years who were just trying to take her for a ride. Looking for a freebie. This woman, however, had a baby. And Audi felt sorry for what she was seeing. Who knows why she needed a room late at night? She could have been running from an abusive situation. Audi again could relate as she remembered the times her mother would tell her there could come a night when she needed to pack quickly and run away with her. Audi wished, more times than she could count, that her mother would have been brave enough to run. Audi would have gone with her in a heartbeat. In fact, her mother was never aware, but Audi always kept a small suitcase already packed underneath her bed. Just in case.

Gran was already asleep upstairs for the night, so whatever Audi decided to do about this guest and her baby was her own decision.

"I have fifty-eight dollars," the young woman said, reaching into the front pocket of her frayed white denim shorts, and she retrieved a wad of crumpled up bills.

"I'll charge you forty for the night. You can pay half now, and the rest when you leave," Audi suggested, already deciding she was going to pay the difference for the room fee out of her own pocket.

"Thank you." Her response seemed genuine, and the baby began to fuss in her arms.

"Your baby is beautiful. What's her name?" Audi asked, taking one twenty-dollar bill from her.

"Jane." the woman replied, and Audi smiled. She liked the name Jane. In fact, when Ben crinkled up his nose at the suggestion, she ignored him and named their baby girl Berkley Jane anyway.

"We don't have a crib to offer you," Audi spoke, talking business again.

"That's okay," she replied. "She always sleeps with me anyway." The baby didn't even have a crib of her own. Audi wondered if she had a home. *Now she was thinking crazy. And it was none of her business.* She remembered Gran's warning to be polite with their guests, but to keep them at arm's length. *She certainly failed to follow that protocol with Wes.*

Audi handed the young woman the key for the second room on the left. She had paid with cash, so Audi didn't even know her name, just Baby Jane's. "There's food and drinks in the kitchen.

And breakfast will be ready during the eight o'clock hour." Audi saw a diaper bag hanging on the young woman's shoulder. She assumed the baby still took formula, or breast milk. "Up the stairs, second room on the left," Audi told her.

"Thanks," she replied, bouncing her fussy baby in her arms. She looked unattached to her child though, Audi thought. She didn't really try to soothe her, and the baby only cried harder. As she walked away, the crying continued. Audi was grateful they had no other guests there tonight. A fussy baby, crying loudly, would be a serious disruption. *She would probably feel obligated to hand out more discounted priced rooms in the morning.* Audi momentarily contemplated going upstairs to Gran's floor, to wake her for a minute to tell her they have a guest with a baby. *It could be a long night.*

Chapter 20

The B&B was quiet when Audi closed her eyes on the couch bed a few minutes after eleven. She still hated sleeping in there alone. She, once again, fell asleep missing her little girl.

By two-thirty in the morning, Audi was startled awake. It took her a minute to come to her senses. A baby was crying. She quickly glanced at the monitor, but the feed was from Gran's room, and she was motionless in her bed. *Oh right,* Audi remembered their guests. *The young woman and Baby Jane.*

The crying didn't cease. It only became louder. And even louder. The cries were very intense. The baby was obviously hungry. Audi got out of bed and grabbed for her robe on the chair in the den.

She walked up the stairs and could hardly stand the ear-piercing cries coming from that floor. She kept walking, and made her way up to Gran's floor. She slowly opened Gran's door and peeked inside. It was dark and she could not tell if Gran was awake or not.

"I'm awake…" Gran spoke aloud. "Who the Sam hell can sleep with that racket going on? I take it we got a guest last night?"

"Yes, just a few minutes before closing, a young woman and her baby arrived."

"Jesus, feed that baby already!" Gran barked. "It's been a long time since I've heard that sound in my house in the wee hours."

"Not as long for me," Audi spoke, feeling sad again. *Six years. That's all she got with her baby girl.*

Gran wished she had not said that, but she reminded herself that not talking about Berkley was absurd – because Audi would always be thinking of her regardless.

"Should I knock on their door? You know, just to check to see if the baby needs anything?"

"We don't do that in this business, Audi girl. That's their private quarters for the night."

"I understand, but geez that crying sounds dire…"

"Let's give it some time. The baby will calm down."

Gran was wrong. Thirty-three minutes passed and the crying only became more hysterical. Audi was seated in the chair beside Gran's bed. Gran was sitting up, and fed up.

"Go!" Gran told her. "Go knock on that damn door." Audi got up and hustled out of the room. Gran didn't have to tell her twice.

Audi went down one flight of stairs to the second floor and made her way to the room with the screaming baby. She knocked once, and waited. She knocked again, and waited. She called through the closed door, "It's Audi. We met earlier tonight!" She couldn't even hear herself talk. "Is everything okay?" she yelled louder through the closed door.

Finally, she tried the door handle and it was unlocked. She turned it, and slowly pushed it open. The bed was unmade and no one was in it. The baby was lying flat on her back on the floor, red faced, tear soaked. Screaming. Choking on its sobs. With her arms and legs frantically flailing. Audi ran to the bathroom and it was empty. She gave the room another once-over. *No mother. Holy shit!*

Audi landed on her knees on the hardwood floor in front of the baby. She picked her up. The white onezie she wore was urine-soaked. She got to her feet, holding the baby, and her cries lessened a notch, but she was still breathless and sobbing. She rushed over to the diaper bag on the dresser top and in it she found a can of formula and one bottle that looked as if it was already mixed. Chancing that it was still safe for the baby, she gave it a shake, removed the cap, and tipped the baby back in her arms and she went after the nipple on that bottle as if she were starv-ed.

Audi stood there, with her back up against the dresser. She could feel the wetness from the saturated diaper, soaking onto the sleeve of her robe. All she wanted to do was feed this baby and give her a warm bath. She glanced in the diaper bag for clean clothes. There wasn't much at all. *Where the hell was this baby's mother?*

The bottle was gone in no time. And when Audi positioned the baby upright in her arms, she immediately burp-ed. "Oh my, Janey," Audi called her, "that was easy." Audi grabbed a fresh diaper from the bag, and a clean onezie. She layed the baby down on the bed to change her. A proper bath would have to wait until her mother returned.

Baby Jane had finally stopped whimpering halfway through taking the bottle, and now she cooed when Audi spoke to her in a high-pitched voice. "Yes, you were hungry. Yes, you were. Now, you feel better, don't you? No more tears. Mommy will be back real soon."

Audi threw the wet diaper in the trash can by the door, and placed the soaked onezie on the floor near it. She cradled the baby as she ascended the stairs up to Gran's room again. Gran was pacing near the foot end of her bed. "Look who I found all alone," Audi spoke, and Gran's eyes widened.

"Please tell me her mother ran out to get milk or some-thing for this baby."

The One You're Waiting On

"The diaper bag was left behind, but that's all she came in with. No luggage."

"We have to call the police," Gran stated.

"Already? What if she comes back in a few minutes? That will cause trouble, because she left the baby alone."

"Exactly. She needs to face the consequences of her actions!" Gran was adamant, and then she glanced at the baby with big, round, brown eyes, smiling with only gums, as her chubby arms and legs were flailing. "You're a pretty little thing, aren't you?" It was obvious to anyone she was a girl because of her pierced ears. Those tiny little gold balls stood out when all she had on her head was half-inch-long white peach fuzz.

"She was screaming in there because she was hungry – and alone. Dammit Gran, we left her cry." Audi felt terrible.

"Well we didn't know. She seems alright now."

"I fed her a bottle that was in the diaper bag, and I changed her. We may need to tend to the mattress in that room later, because this baby was pee soaked." Audi was unsure if the baby had been on the bed prior to when she found her on the floor next to it.

Gran nodded her head. That was just another reason why she had sealed each mattress in that B&B in protective plastic covers. "Was she on that big bed by herself?" Gran thought of the high-off-the-floor king sized beds in each of the six rooms.

"No, she was on the floor when I walked in."

"Jesus, she probably fell off the bed! Maybe she hit her head on that hard floor? The police may need to have her checked out at Anderson."

"Seriously?" Audi asked. "She doesn't need to go to the hospital." Just the thought of that hospital made Audi cringe. One fall from the swing in the yard had led to an x-ray, a cancer diagnosis, an MRI, emergency surgery, and then her daughter died. *It was fucking unreal. And unfair.*

Audi forced her thoughts on the baby in her arms. "Okay, call the police, Gran, but no hospital." Baby Jane was comfortable in Audi's arms, as she chewed on the terrycloth drawstring from the hood of her robe. Drool was dripping from her chubby little chin.

Chapter 21

An officer from the Maryville Police Department showed up, and Audi was still in her robe with the baby in one arm as she opened the door. Gran sat back on the sofa in the sitting room.

After a series of questions, Audi had not been much help. She didn't know what type of vehicle the woman was driving. It was dark outside when she arrived – and still dark when she left. She paid cash, and never had a reason to give a name. She had only said the baby's name was Jane. And that may not even have been true. Even still, Audi had been touched. The officer asked to take a look around the room the young mother rented for the night. When the officer was upstairs, Audi walked around the room with Baby Jane. She liked movement and just looking around. She had not cried at all since Audi rescued her alone in that room upstairs, and had fed and changed her. She tended to her needs, just as her mother should be doing right now.

"We have no name, nothing to go on," Gran stated, from the end of the sofa.

"I know. As you heard me tell the officer, she paid cash." Audi thought of the twenty dollars she charged her, and she looked down at the check-in desk and was surprised to see another folded up twenty dollar bill. That was not the one from last night, Audi was certain. She picked it up, and in the corner of the bill someone had written in blue ink pen, *thank you.*

Thank you for what? Audi thought to herself. *You left without your baby!*

Gran was watching her. "What is it, Audi girl?"

"She left this baby behind. Abandoned her." Audi looked down at the baby turning her head from side to side.

"That was my first thought upstairs when you told me she was left alone in that room."

"Not mine. I had hope, I believed she was coming back."

"You always did give everyone the benefit of the doubt."

"What will happen to her now?" Audi held the baby closer for a long moment.

"Foster care."

"Gran, that's awful," Audi sighed, as the officer descended the stairs. He was already through with his search.

Before he spoke, Audi did. "I need to tell you something." She went on to explain how she only charged the young woman forty dollars, and accepted twenty from her last night.

Audi handed the officer the second twenty dollar bill that she had just found on the desk.

"It says, thank you," Audi pointed out, and the officer flipped the bill over to the backside, and then to the front side again. "Do you think she abandoned her baby here last night?" Audi asked the officer.

"It looks that way, yes."

"What will happen to her now?"

"She'll go with child protective services, and end up in foster care if we aren't able to track down who she belongs to. In cases like this, hopefully, eventually, the baby will be adopted. It's unfortunate, but it's the way this works." The officer seemed sympathetic, but accustomed, to the situation.

"What if I keep her for awhile? You know, maybe just until you track down her mother or some family?" Audi sug--gested, and Gran found herself wanting to protest. She caught herself though before she did. *Audi was going to get too attached to that baby, only to see it be taken away. Or, this may just be what she needs right now to heal.* Gran held her tongue, and hoped to God this was going to turn out well.

"Child Protective Services must be contacted, but I don't see why you cannot be a temporary caregiver. Talk to them. It's very selfless of you to want to care for this baby until we have some answers."

"It's something I need to do," Audi heard herself say aloud, and Gran watched her closely with that child in her arms.

Audi didn't wait around for Child Protective Services to show up. By the time Nurse Jo was walking into the B&B to work, Audi was headed out of the door with a baby in her arms. *Gran will explain*, was all she said as she passed her. Nurse Jo squeezed the baby's hand and could hardly wait to speak to Gran.

Audi had given Baby Jane a warm bath, and put on a one-piece yellow seersucker outfit. There was only one other outfit left in the diaper bag. The can of formula was still half full, and she had taken the entire diaper bag with her when she left. She would need to buy more of everything in it – the formula, the diapers, and clothes.

But, first, as Audi reached her car, she realized she needed a car seat to transport her in. Already having to think on her feet, and think of everything, Audi walked down the drive and across the street. The neighbor guy was mowing his front lawn, and he shut off the engine as soon as he saw her walking toward him with a baby in her arms. He knew Gran well, and had gotten to know Audi when his son Colsen played with Berkley. His heart broke for this woman and the loss of her sweet little girl. He saw the baby in her arms, but had no idea who she belonged to.

"Audi, everything all right?" Colsen's father spoke, with sincerity and concern in his voice. Audi knew Colsen had a younger sister, maybe thirteen months old, and she hoped they still had her infant car seat.

The One You're Waiting On

"I need a favor," Audi began. "Do you still have Quinn's infant car seat? This baby was left at the B&B last night, and is in need of some things, so I'm taking her shopping."

"Unbelievable," Colsen's father responded, realizing that was why the police car was parked over there for awhile very early this morning. "And, yes, we just switched out from the infant seat, but still have it in the garage. I'll get it and install it for you." *My, my, sometimes things did work effortlessly in her favor.*

~

Audi spent three hours shopping at the stores on Route 159 in Edwardsville. She found more than enough clothes at Old Navy and Kohl's. At Target, she bought formula, diapers, baby toys, and a portable pack-n-play for her to sleep in. Audi sat in the car and fed Jane a bottle before finally heading back to the B&B. Audi realized what was happening. She told herself not to analyze or overthink this. Even it if was only for a little while, she relished this feeling of having a purpose again.

Audi carefully placed the sleeping baby down on a quilt on the living room floor. All that shopping had worn her out. Gran sat on the end of the sofa, watching the baby sleep, while Audi and Nurse Jo made three or four trips back and forth from the car to retrieve all her purchases.

"This is a lot of stuff for a baby you don't know how long you'll have," Nurse Jo spoke carefully, and Gran shot her a look of disapproval. They had discussed this as being good for Audi right now, but agreed she was indeed putting her heart on the line. Gran had said she wanted to wait this out, and not steer Audi in any particular direction.

"It is," Audi agreed, "but she came with practically nothing. If I'm going to take care of her, I need the stuff to do it."

"But for how long?" Nurse Jo pressed, and Gran never interjected into this conversation. She was, however, just as concerned as Nurse Jo.

"I don't know. I can send this stuff with her, if she has to go," Audi stated, and she seemed perfectly content with the possibility. And Nurse Jo was just as pleased with her answer. *At least Audi was not disconnected from reality. And the reality of this circumstance was…that baby may not permanently stay there.*

Chapter 22

Child Protective Services agreed to allow Audi to provide a temporary home for the baby. She had to fill out endless paperwork to start the process, but for now she had custody of a baby without a full name, birth date, or any information regarding who and where she came from. Again, Audi was reminded that her offer to help care for the baby was only temporary.

Audi was told that the baby's mother still had rights to her child, even though she abandoned it. If she changed her mind and returned, she would have to go through court proceedings to regain custody. Eventually, if she did not return, the mother's rights would be terminated, and the baby would be eligible for adoption. It was standard procedure for Child Protective Services to go over those details with anyone who found an abandoned infant and wanted to take any responsibility to care for it, whether it was temporary or permanent.

Audi also learned if the police were unable to locate Baby Jane's parents, she would become a ward of the state, and the state would automatically take custody. Just like that, the search for the mother would cease. Efforts to contact a non-surrendering parent, such as Jane's father, would also be made.

Audi knew there were laws and she could not just keep the baby she found. That was precisely why she told the Child Protective Services employee that she wanted to be the baby's temporary legal guardian. And she signed the necessary paperwork to document that. Even with temporary guardianship, Audi was told the baby could still be taken away from her at any time. Unless she chose to submit a request for formal adoption. Audi never responded to that. That was too much too soon. Temporary guardianship seemed safer for the time being. She still believed the mother would return for her baby.

~

The One You're Waiting On

It was midnight before Audi settled into bed. To say it had been a productive day would be an understatement. She rolled over onto her side and looked at the pack-n-play set up beside her. Jane was sound asleep and had been for hours. She would get to know her schedule. *Did she still wake up in the middle of the night to have a bottle?* Since she had the night before, at half past two in the morning, Audi was prepared for much of the same. Only this time, she wouldn't have to cry so long before she was fed and comforted.

Audi rolled over, onto her back after she retrieved her cell phone from the desk near the bed. She hadn't checked her messages all day. Not that she cared if anyone had tried to contact her. But she did take a look now.

There were four text messages. One was from Ben. She didn't know how she felt about him anymore. *Hi. This sucks. I think of Berk night and day.* Audi swallowed hard, and tears immediately pooled in her eyes. *Call me. We need to discuss our divorce.* Only Ben could toy with her emotions like that. One minute she felt his pain, and the next minute he was thinking of only himself and how he wanted out of their marriage. *It was probably at Phoebe's urging.*

The second message was from, *speak of the devil*, Phoebe. *Call me. I know I'm a bitch and so much more. Please call. I'm worried about you.* Audi clicked out of that message, and thought, *yes, a bitch and so much more.*

A third message was from the lawyer's office she had contacted weeks ago. She would call that number in the morning. It was time to finalize everything with her husband. She didn't have a husband anymore anyway.

The fourth, and final message, forced her heartbeat to quicken. It was from Wes. Audi rolled over onto her stomach on the bed and began to read it.

Hey there…Remember me? I'm thinking of you. Not that I've ever stopped. You're not someone who crosses my mind now and then. You're there all the time. I think you know I care. I cannot imagine your unbearable pain, but I have a damn good idea of it after being there with you. I just want you to know that I left because you forced me to. If you asked me to come back, I would stop at nothing to get to you. Ask me to come back.

Signed,

Uncomfortably numb right now

Audi smiled. And then she reread his text. He hadn't given up on her. Like Gran said, there were going to be blessings in her life. She just needed to open her heart to them. Audi took her eyes off of her phone and looked over at the sleeping baby. Jane was a blessing, no matter if she was only in her life temporarily. And, as for Wes, she replied to his text message.

Thank you for thinking of me, Delahunt.

Signed,

I couldn't forget you if I tried.

~

The One You're Waiting On

Since the B&B was vacant, Audi asked Nurse Jo to watch the baby for an hour, because the following day she already had an appointment with a lawyer. While at the lawyer's office, Audi didn't have any other choice but to contact Ben. The lawyer she just hired wanted to know the name of her husband's lawyer and what was drawn up on his behalf. Audi's lawyer needed to know what kind of fight, if any, he was in for.

The lawyer stepped out his office when Audi called Ben. He answered on the second ring. "Audi?"

"Ben. I'm at my lawyer's office. I just hired him today. I'll be honest, I have no clue what you want from me, or what your lawyer has in writing for us to agree on. I don't want this to be some nasty, ongoing battle. My goal isn't to take you to the cleaners, as they say, because you broke your marriage vows. All I want is out. I think I'm entitled to something." Audi swallowed hard when she thought of how Ben no longer needed to provide child support. A month ago, that would have been Audi's only concern. Her sole reason to fight him.

Just listening to her speak, reminded him why he loved her from the moment he met her. She was real. One of the good ones. A rare woman. And he was a fool for messing things up. "Get the fax number there at your lawyer's, and I will send over a copy of our divorce papers." He didn't say he hoped she would think he was being more than fair. He only listened until Audi found out the number, once she walked out of the office and into the lobby where the receptionist was working.

"Thanks for calling," Ben said to her, when he knew she was ready to end their phone call.

"Thanks for faxing. I guess I'll have my lawyer call your lawyer." She smiled a little, even though she felt sad.

"You can call me yourself," he offered.

"Okay," she responded and then ended their connection.

When Audi's lawyer returned, he was holding the faxed copy of the divorce papers.

"So? How bad is it?" she asked, cautiously.

"It's surprising," he answered. "Your husband wants you to have half of everything. What you don't sell, he said is yours. He only wants his car and his golf clubs. And," the lawyer cleared his throat, "there was a savings account in place at the bank for your now deceased daughter." The lawyer paused because he had watched her face fall. "He wants you to have it all. Apparently her college fund was already in place." This was a surprise to Audi. She knew Ben had started a savings account for their baby girl the day she was born. But, she had no idea Berkley's daddy had taken such good care of her future. A future that was no more. The tears pooled in her eyes in front of a complete stranger. It couldn't be helped. That's what happened when she thought of Berkley and what might have been. And that's what probably always would happen. It just hurt that much.

"I'm sorry," she apologized, trying to pull herself together.

"Don't be," her lawyer spoke. "Just sign this. You deserve it. Unless you want me to fight for something specific, or for more money?"

"No, that won't be necessary," Audi told him, as she wiped her tear-soaked cheeks with back of her hand.

When she left, she got into her car. She sat there behind the wheel, and once again called Ben.

"Are you okay with it?" he spoke as he answered.

"I am," she told him. "I never wanted to fight you."

"I know that," he said to her. "I also never meant to hurt you, if you will ever believe that." Ben closed his eyes on the opposite end of the phone.

"You did though," she replied. "But what does it matter now? I think we both will hurt more than enough for the rest of our lives because we lost our Berkley. There's no need to add to our pain. Just try to have a good life, Ben."

This time it was Ben whose face was tear soaked. Audi could hear him choking on his words when he finally did reply. "A good life was what I had."

"Goodbye Ben."

"Take care of yourself, Audi Pence." He had to say it one last time. Her name. With his last name. Because he knew a woman like her would in no time find another man who wanted to love her and marry her. And give her his name.

Chapter 23

Audi returned to the B&B feeling taken aback. How had she gone from just hiring a lawyer to finalizing everything with Ben? It seemed too easy, and entirely too final. But that was life sometimes, as she had learned in the most excruciating way when she lost Berkley. Nothing, not a damn thing, was forever. And just like that, anyone's entire world, reason for living and loving, could vanish.

She stepped into the B&B to hear squeals from Baby Jane. She was sitting up, propped with the boppy pillow Audi had bought for her. Nurse Jo was close by on the floor, making the baby squeal with a game of peek-a-boo. Audi smiled. Nurse Jo looked like a proud grandmother.

"Looks like she was no bother," Audi quipped.

"She's such a joy," Nurse Jo said, struggling to get up off of the floor from her knees to her feet.

"I don't understand how her mother could just leave her," Audi said, feeling so far from comprehending how any mother could condone giving up her child. There were valid reasons, she tried to believe. But after having no choice when she lost Berkley, Audi now wholeheartedly believed a mother should do anything, and everything, possible to be with her child. Always.

"We don't know her situation," Nurse Jo defended.

"True, but still," Audi stated, as she swept up Baby Jane into her arms and planted a kiss on her chubby little cheek, as if she were resting her case. *But still, look at this beautiful innocent baby.*

~

By late afternoon, both the baby and Gran were napping at the same time. Nurse Jo was in the kitchen preparing something that made Audi hungry just taking in the scent of it when she stepped out of the front door and onto the wraparound porch. It had been a day or two since she made her way out to that swing.

She held onto those same old rusty chains as she sat down on the bendy rubber. *Hey Berk...*she said aloud. *Mommy misses you like crazy. If I let it –this feeling, the pain of losing you– would drive me there. Straight to crazyland. I can't let it though, can I?* She paused and released her feet from resting on the ground. The swing took her forward, and then back. *I hope there are swings in heaven for you. I hope you've met Grandma Monica. Ask her to push you. Not too high though. You could fall.* Audi cried openly when she said those words. *Yes, she could fall. And she had. And then everything spiraled out of control. And Audi's life forever changed.*

Audi cried for awhile on that swing, and then finally she regained her composure. She knew she needed to go back inside and listen for the baby to wake up. She also knew Nurse Jo was dependable and would take care of her for a little while. As she contemplated getting off of that swing, she saw a vehicle turn into the drive. She only thought for a second that it could be a customer, before she recognized that expensive white Mercedes. How many times had she not seen it cruising through their Tower Grove South subdivision, straight down their street and into the garage directly across the street.

Audi wanted to roll her eyes. It wasn't exactly subtle of Phoebe to come there just hours after she and Ben had unofficially finalized their divorce over the phone. Audi stayed where she was on the swing.

As always, Phoebe shined in white denim capris, heeled silver sandals, and a teal satin oxford blouse, unbuttoned entirely too low. Her hair was down and blowing in the wind. Audi couldn't have cared less what her own curls looked like right now in the humid air, but she ran her fingers through them anyway. Maybe she had always felt somewhat insecure around her best friend who was more beautiful and sexier than most women.

Audi never spoke as Phoebe stopped walking when she reached the swingset, and stood about ten feet away from her. "I know I'm the last person on earth you want to see," she began, and Audi cut her off.

"Yep, pretty much."

"I'm staying with Drake." Drake was Phoebe's husband who had been deployed to China for three months for his government job.

"Is that fair to him when you're getting naked with my husband?" Audi didn't care anymore. This woman betrayed her in the worst way. She didn't have any love or respect left for her, nor would she ever again want her in her life.

"We ended it," Phoebe stated.

"Poor Ben," Audi said sarcastically.

"Drake doesn't know," Phoebe began speaking again.

"Oh, so that's why you're here? You want me to keep my mouth shut, so you can keep your happy little home life? Wow, you made out pretty good with that deal. Ben lost everything –

all for fucking you. And now, you will quietly slip back into your life – and he's left with nothing."

"He would take you back, you know that."

"I don't want him back. He's used goods now, thanks to you."

"I didn't come here to beg you not to go to Drake."

"I don't care about you or your marriage," Audi spat back at her.

"I never meant to hurt you," Phoebe spoke, and to Audi it was the shallowest thing she had ever heard. Ben had said the same thing to her, but even his words had not affected her the way Phoebe's had. She assumed it was because another woman, a friend who she bonded with like a sister, should never cross a line like that. Not if they really loved and respected each other.

"No? But you got what you wanted, Phoebs!" Audi paused for a moment, debating whether or not to speak her mind, or just let it go. She decided fairly quickly that she had absolutely nothing to lose. "I'm the one you told, most of, your secrets to, remember? I know about the other two affairs you've had during your marriage. I never judged you. You know that. Not until you hunted and hooked my husband. You're a whore. Poor Drake. He will have to find that out for himself someday. He will not hear it from me. Yeah, you see, I'm the loyal friend."

"I suppose I deserved that," Phoebe said, still standing in the tall grass in front of Audi. She started to turn around, as if she was prepared to walk away, as if she really had come there only to ensure Drake would never find out she had cheated on him with Neighbor Ben. What Audi wouldn't have given to be able to cry in her once best friend's arms. But that woman before her now was not the dear friend she believed her to be. Phoebe turned back to Audi one last time. "I'm not a whore," she defended herself.

"No?" Audi was surprised her words had even affected Phoebe.

"He touched me like he loved me. We didn't just have sex. We made passionate love. And his kisses were absolutely intoxicating."

Audi suppressed the need to call her *a bitch* again. But, she did speak her mind through a clenched jaw. "Get out of here. You can drive off the Poplar Street Bridge, for all I care. I never want to see you again."

Audi left the swing and made her way back inside of the B&B before Phoebe even had the chance to drive off.

Goodbye friend.

Chapter 24

For one week, Audi took exceptional, loving care of Jane. She was reminded of the spit up, the dirty diapers, the sleepless nights, and never having enough hours in a day to get anything done. But, most of all, she was given the chance to relive how precious it was to care for and love a baby. For herself, Audi wished this would never end. She wanted to keep Jane, eventually adopt her, and raise her. But she tried to be realistic. This baby girl could have family out there, worried about her, and begging for her safe return.

When Audi heard the ding of the bell above the front door at the B&B, she walked from kitchen, with Jane in her arms, to greet their guest. And then she recognized the nice woman from Child Protective Services and the officer from the Maryville Police Department who responded to their emergency call the night Jane was abandoned at the B&B.

"I'm afraid to speculate why you're here..." Audi spoke first and the baby cooed in her arms. The sunlight coming through the front windows always caught Jane's attention. She wasn't the least bit concerned about the strangers in the foyer. But Audi was.

"We tracked down who the baby belongs to," the officer spoke gently. He knew Audi's story. Everyone in that town did. And the idea of her starting over, beginning again by rescuing a baby that needed love and care, was storybook. "Her father lives in Troy..." Troy was an adjacent city to Maryville, just six miles away, "and he wants full custody of her."

Audi inhaled a deep breath through her nostrils. She held Jane a little closer and cinched her arms tighter around her chubby little body. She was getting fuller, and that was most likely because she was eating well. "And what about her mother?" Audi wanted to know. She needed to know.

"Missing still," the officer informed her. "The baby does have other family, besides her father, who may be willing to help care for her."

"It's time to give her back," the woman from Child Protective Services spoke cautiously. She had seen cases like this turn ugly. Attachments were formed quickly. And it was difficult to say goodbye after falling in love with a child.

"I have formula, diapers, toys, oh and the pack-n-play set up in my bedroom – that's where she sleeps. All of her clothes, too!" Audi was rambling. Nervously. This couldn't be goodbye. Nurse Jo and Gran filed out of the kitchen and stood close to her and the baby. Audi felt Gran's hand rubbing her back, repeatedly. "She has an appointment at the pediatrician here in town next week. I guess I could cancel that. I'm sure her father will take good care of her, and give her what she needs." Audi kissed the baby girl on her ear as she turned her little head into her.

"I'll gather her things," Nurse Jo offered, hanging her head as she walked away. The officer and the woman stepped back when Gran asked for a minute alone with Audi and the child. They heard the officer say they would wait outside on the front porch. They needed to make sure no attempt would be made to escape with the baby.

Audi was crying before the front door was closed behind them. "Now, now," Gran told her, as Audi clutched the baby closer to her and repeatedly kissed the top of her fuzzy little head. "This has to be. You knew it was possible."

She nodded her head through her tears, and Baby Jane grabbed a handful of blonde curls, covering the side of Audi's face. "God must hate me," Audi said, choking on a sob.

"I've been there, and felt the very same way, Audi girl." That's what Audi loved so much about Gran. She got it. She understood everything.

"If you were so sure this would happen, why didn't you try to prepare me better?" Audi asked, suddenly feeling like a child who needed guidance, who could pass off the responsibility onto someone else.

"Because I know how much you needed this. If only for a little while." Gran didn't have to say anymore. Audi shook her head in agreement, and kissed Jane one more time. The baby's drool was now on Audi's lips and both she and Gran smiled. "Remember when I told you to open your heart to new blessings? Well, here you have one."

"I know, I see that. But again, I have to, no I'm forced to, give up one of my greatest blessings. Gran, it's just not fair!"

"No, it's not at all fair. Be strong. Maybe ask the officer and the woman outside if they will give Jane's father your contact information. You could stay in touch, check up on her once in awhile, or maybe…" Gran paused, hesitating whether or not to speak it. "Maybe if he cannot raise his baby, he will turn to you, knowing you can."

Audi smiled. "I will tuck the hope for that into my heart's pocket."

The two of them, along with Baby Jane, walked to the back of the house on the main level and into the den to help Nurse Jo gather everything that needed to go home with Baby Jane. When they returned to the sitting area near the check-in desk, it was time.

The officer made two trips back and forth from his car and the woman's car outside. It was obvious how much Audi loved that baby and how well taken care of she was there. A baby abandoned with practically nothing was leaving there with so much. Especially love.

Audi wasn't strong enough. She just didn't have it in her to do this. She held Jane up a little higher and turned her around, nose to nose with her. "I love you, Janey. Tell your daddy to take very good care of you." The tears were pouring out of Audi's eyes and dripping off of her face as she quickly handed the baby over to Gran. And then she abruptly walked away without making any attempt to look back.

~

She was back there again. Back to that place where the world felt dark and cold and lonely. Audi wanted to go outside and sit on the swing, but it was nightfall and leaving her room in the den right now did not appeal to her. Both Gran and Nurse Jo had taken their turns coming in to check on her, but she made it clear each time that she only wanted to be left alone. She would come out of this again, Audi knew. She just needed time. Time to think about that baby…and Berkley. And how much she would love and miss those baby girls for the rest of her life. And then after her tears were gone again, Audi would think of all the good they brought into her life. Even if it was only for a little while.

When Gran walked Nurse Jo out, after another day at the B&B, she locked the door of the inn early. She didn't want to deal with any customers tonight. She just wanted to shut the place down, turn off all of the lights, and go to bed. Tomorrow would be another day. As she walked past the check-in desk, she noticed Audi's cell phone had been left there.

Gran was technically challenged, but she did know a little about how to work a cell phone. In fact, Berkley had showed her a few new things she was unfamiliar with on her own cell phone that she had for years.

Gran didn't believe in interfering with fate or destiny, or any sort of matchmaking. But, this just felt dire. She feared Audi was at the end of her rope. And she really could not blame her. Life had beaten her down, and continued to repeatedly knock the wind out of her.

She found Audi's contact list. She didn't know how to text. She could only make phone calls. She preferred to talk to people anyway. Words on a screen could be misinterpreted. She wanted Wes to hear her voice and understand how important it was for him to come back. If that's what he truly wanted to do.

In fear of being overheard, Gran unlocked the front door again, flipped on the porch lights, and walked outside just as Wes answered on the third ring.

"Audi?"

"No, it's her Gran."

"Oh, hello. Did something happen to Audi?" Wes felt panic rise in his chest, and he momentarily held his breath.

Chapter 25

It was barely lunch time and Nurse Jo would not stop harping about her craving for ice cream at Bobby's Frozen Custard on Route 159. "Come on, Miss Audi, don't you want to drive up there and get something sinful?"

"Not really," Audi said, looking at Gran from across the table. Gran laughed out loud as Audi rolled her eyes.

"When a craving hits, you gotta feed it," Gran said, nodding her head and egging on Nurse Jo.

"Ugh, you two are driving me bananas!" Audi spoke out, feeling irritated but she did enjoy their company and the fact that they were keeping her mind on something else, finally something trivial.

"A banana split! That's it! That's what I want!" Nurse Jo exclaimed, pushing her chair back from the kitchen table and using both of her hands to push off of the tabletop when she stood upright.

"Bring me one back, will ya?" Gran asked. "I'll stay here and hold down the fort. Go on, Audi. Drive Nurse Jo up there." *Couldn't Nurse Jo drive herself?* Despite the objections she wanted to make, Audi gave in. She picked up her cell phone and car keys off of the counter, and then she left the kitchen mumbling something about needing to grab her handbag.

Gran and Nurse Jo exchanged glances – and winks. "I'll need at least thirty minutes," Gran told her, and Nurse Jo gave her the okay sign with her hand.

~

Audi had never seen anyone eat ice cream slower than Nurse Jo. After almost ten minutes of debating between that banana split she was so certain she wanted and a turtle sundae, Nurse Jo finally ordered the banana split. Audi sipped a vanilla milkshake to appease Nurse Jo. But really all she wanted to do was go back to the B&B and hide in her room. She missed Janey. What a pleasant, perfect distraction she had been. And certainly so much more.

Forty-five minutes after they left to get ice cream, Audi was finally driving them back to the B&B. Nurse Jo was smiling in the passenger seat beside her, as she held Gran's to-go banana split on her lap. Audi felt like rolling her eyes, as she hoped when she grew old she would have more than ice cream to excite her like that.

When they drove up to the B&B, there was a strange car parked there. "Looks like we have another guest," Audi commented, and Nurse Jo replied, "Sure does."

Nurse Jo followed Audi into the B&B. She watched Audi's face when they stepped into the foyer and Gran was standing there with Wes. He was wearing jeans and a t-shirt Audi had not seen before. He looked different, but so very much the same.

"Aren't you going to say anything?" Wes asked her as both Gran and Nurse Jo looked on. "Don't you people have a special warm welcome for guests who return?"

Audi smiled at him and took a few steps closer to him. Wes opened his arms to her and she practically fell into his embrace. Wes held her like only he could. With intensity, with affection, and with love. Audi could feel how much he loved her. She never wanted to push him away, but she believed she had to. She still wasn't sure why he came back, or what she could truly offer him at this stage in her life, where her world continued to feel as if it was crumbling.

They pulled apart but stood close. "How long are you staying here this time?" she partly teased him, but did want to know.

"Oh I'm not staying. Just passing through this time."

The One You're Waiting On

"Okay," Audi didn't know what else to say. *Why would he be in the area? Possibly to finally finish writing his book? And, more importantly, why would he torture her with only a brief hello and goodbye?* She was sick and tired of goodbyes and felt both miffed and defeated knowing this.

"I'm driving back to Utah today, tonight, all night long. It's a long ways." Wes spoke seriously. "I flew into St. Louis an hour ago, rented that car parked outside, and now I'm here to get what I came for and go back home."

Audi was confused and her expression showed it. "That's extreme. What in the world did you come here to pick up?"

"You," Wes spoke, and took both of her hands in his. Gran and Nurse Jo stepped back and joined each other side by side on the opposite end of the check-in desk.

Audi looked at them both. "You two! You both knew about this? Your ridiculous ice cream craving was some sort of stall tactic! You're both crazy." Audi smiled at them, and Gran spoke.

"Audi girl, you're all packed. Your bags are already in the trunk of Wes' car. Go. Be. I have Nurse Jo here to tag team this place. You need this. You must do something for you before all that's happened consumes you." Gran had said as much to Wes on the phone last night too when she explained the baby story to him. She wasn't sure how much more heartache and loss Audi could take.

"I love you so much, Gran. You too, Nurse Jo! And you," she looked at Wes, "I want to run with you right now, I do. I just don't know how long I can keep running away. That's not the answer."

"Understand something," he told her. "You will not be running away from anything. Together we will be running to something, something pretty damn wonderful if you ask me what I foresee." Audi touched his face. It was scruffy again. "We will be back, I promise. Do not tell these two wonderful women goodbye. Just say see you soon..."

That's what sold her on doing it, just going for it. Knowing she didn't have to say another goodbye. That, and the beautiful fact that she loved this man.

She nodded her head.

"Is that a yes? You'll go with me, back to Utah?" Wes' hopes were sky high at this moment.

Audi leapt into his arms. She wanted to kiss him so badly, but they had an audience. *In due time,* she told herself.

After quick, but meaningful hugs between her and those incredibly special ladies in her life, they were off. Running away. Driving away. Just getting away. Whatever this was, and whatever it would come to be, Audi never felt more ready to just embrace what made her happy. She already had learned more than once in her life how important it was to live in the now.

Chapter 26

They drove all night long, having only stopped for take-out food and drinks, restroom breaks, and to refill the gas tank in the rental car. Their time together fueled the fire of their budding relationship. Although they were just beginning to get to know each other, they already were so closely bonded. When they arrived at Wes' country home the following afternoon, Wes desperately needed sleep. Audi had gotten some rest as Wes drove through the night, but he had never given in to her offer to drive the next morning so he could sleep. He was functioning purely on adrenaline now.

The dust flew around the entire car as they made their way up the narrow lane road that led to his old farm house.

"Are you serious?" Audi asked him, looking out of the car windows at the house and the barn in the distance, and all of the land. "This is incredible. So peaceful. Ahh, just wonderful." Wes was grinning from ear to ear at her. *She loved where he lived. And he loved seeing her look so happy. It was time she was again.*

Wes parked behind that old antique Walton's replica truck. "Is that yours too?" she asked him.

"No, it's my sister's dream vehicle, if you can possibly imagine."

"So she's here?" Audi felt mildly disappointed as she was looking forward to finally being alone with him. Falling into bed. To sleep first. And then hopefully much more.

"Yes, she's here to meet you. I know what that seems like, but you'll soon understand. And after the two of you talk, I'll kick her out." Wes laughed and Audi tried to. But she felt uncomfortable not being prepared or knowing what to expect.

Wes carried Audi's luggage and just a backpack of his own. They stepped up onto the front porch and a woman, almost as tall as Wes, with those same bright green eyes, swung open the door for them.

"Nice to be greeted so warmly at my own house," Wes teased, as his sister hugged his neck. "Robyn, meet Audi. Audi, this is my big sis, Robyn with a y." The two women giggled and reached for each other's hand.

"It's wonderful to meet you," Robyn said first.

"Oh same here," Audi sincerely agreed.

After a little talk about their long trip, Wes looked at Audi. "I'm going to take a shower if you two want to talk. Robyn chased him off, while Audi wished he would stay.

"He's the best brother I could have ever hoped for," Robyn said when Wes left the room. The ceilings were high inside of that house which resembled a log cabin, fireplace and all.

"I'm an only child, so having a bond with a sibling is foreign to me." Audi explained, and briefly thought of Phoebe and their connection that once felt like the sisterhood she had only heard about.

"My husband can relate to that, too," Robyn offered, while she walked into the kitchen. "Can I get you a drink? I'm sorry, I know you're probably ready to crash, and really wish I wasn't here right now." Audi shook her head as if Robyn's comment could not be farther from the truth. Robyn uncorked a bottle of white wine and Audi didn't object. They each took their full glasses into the living area and sat down on the red sectional. It was one of soft, worn, comfortable leather.

Audi sipped her wine first. "I'm curious what's so important?" she came right out and asked her. And Robyn wasted no time answering.

"I have twin sons. They're two." Audi smiled. Wes had told her all about his rambunctious nephews. "They weren't my first. I had a baby girl who died." Audi grasped tighter the hold she had on her wine glass. A woman with a familiar pain. "She died just two days shy of her first birthday. She had a heart defect, never detected, until it was too late." Audi saw the tears pooling in Wes' sister's eyes. That pain. It never truly goes away.

"I'm sorry," Audi said, and meant it.

"I am too. I'm sorry I was only allocated one year with her. I'm sorry I'm still hurt and angry and overwhelmingly sad at times still. I just want to share with you that, sure, life goes on, if we make a conscious effort to allow it to. But, forgetting or even being successful at tucking their memory away so it can be a little less painful is not doable. I live with the pain, and you will too."

Audi was openly crying now. "I didn't think this trip would be like this. I told myself to tone down the tears for Wes, for the *us* we are trying to find together."

"That's a mistake, if I may just come right out and say it," Robyn spoke without reservation. "I never intended to tell you this, it's not really my place to share it, but it just feels right at this moment – because of what you said. Wes wants to be there for you through everything. God knows he's pulled me out of the quicksand of grief more than anyone else. More than my own husband, who's battling his own grief for our daughter." Audi listened raptly. "We were here, outside on Wes' front porch, when he told me what happened to Berkley." *Just hearing her say Berkley's name filled Audi with an indescribable joy. Because Wes' sister even knew her name. This was what Audi now realized she wanted and needed. Her daughter deserved to be remembered.* "I told him how I used to be one of those mothers, blessed with my child here with me. But now I'm one of them living day to day, sometimes just minute to minute, with the pain and heartbreak from losing a part of me. What Wes said to me tore him up. He said your little girl was the most beautiful with her blonde curls and bright blue eyes…she was a little sassy and a lot sweet. He told me he had fallen for her, too."

Audi put her face in her hands and cried. My goodness, did she ever recognize the blessing of having that man in her life. Now more than ever. He was the one she had been waiting on. And she had not even been conscious of it. Wes came into her life when her commitment to Ben was falling apart, and then, when her world completely shattered as Berkley's body and spirit left this earth. *The one she was waiting on.* Audi had been a fool to push him out of her life.

~

Audi walked into his bedroom. She wasn't even sure which room was located where yet in his house. With Robyn there when they arrived, everything else was on hold. But now, Audi completely understood why his sister needed to speak to her. From the heart. Audi had quickly learned that people share tragedy. Someone, somewhere always knows. Because, others too, have been there and stumbled through similar pain.

Audi stopped in the doorway when she saw him sprawled out on the bed, on his back, sound asleep. He wore only navy blue boxer shorts and his body looked exceptional. Toned. Thick in all the right places. A narrow waist. Long legs with definition. She had to stop staring, afraid she might wake him and she knew how exhausted he was.

Audi spotted her suitcase at the base of the bed. She had absolutely no idea what Gran packed for her so quickly. And she really didn't care. She just wanted something comfortable to slip into after the shower she was longing to take.

She found what she hoped was packed after she toweled off from her soothing, hot shower. Her old and worn Pink Floyd t-shirt and a pair of panties never looked better to her. She laughed to herself because the sexiest man she had ever laid eyes on was asleep on the bed in the next room, and she was slipping into something *old and worn* – just to fall asleep beside him.

When Audi made her way back into his bedroom, Wes stirred in his sleep. He was lying on top of the bedding, so there was no hope of crawling under the covers. Audi moved onto the bed, on the opposite side of him. The mere movement of placing her head on the pillow and curling up her legs as she rolled to her side, facing him, woke him. He opened his eyes, staring at the ceiling, and then he turned to find her staring at him.

"Oh hey…what a shit I am for falling asleep."

She giggled. "Not at all. Just a very tired boy."

"Um, boy?" he asked in a tone that begged to differ.

"Uh huh, boy," she teased.

"Oh, I see… maybe we should clear up that somehow misguided opinion you have of me."

"I'm game," she told him, feeling the heat rise in her body, and settle between her legs.

Wes moved closer. He kissed her slowly, but passionately. She could tell he was eager. Or was that her? Her response to him was like a reflex. It just happened without thinking about it. She didn't want to think anyhow. She just wanted to feel. Everything.

When he made his way on top of her, he looked down at her shirt. And read it. "Are you serious?" he laughed. "How long have you owned yours?"

"Every bit as long as you've had yours."

"And you didn't say anything?" he teasingly chided her.

"What was I supposed to say? I saw your shirt before I saw your amazing green eyes. I might have scared you away if I had said something along the lines of…We are so meant to be together."

Wes' wide smiled faded slowly as he came at her with a force, his lips to hers, that she craved more of. Their open mouths and tongues explored each other's. She was breathless and he was kissing her hard and gentle, fast and slow, all at the same time. He parted from her lips, and looked directly into her eyes. He never said a word, and neither did she. He only reached for the hem of her shirt and rolled it up and off of her body. Her perky breasts were bare, and he touched her nipples with his fingers first. Then with his whole hands. And then with his lips and tongue he took great desire in tasting her. Sucking her until she ached everywhere. She tightened as he moved his hand inside of her panties. She had never felt more desired by any man. And he could feel how much she wanted him. Her panties came off abruptly. She may have helped him remove them faster. He slid his finger inside of her and she arched her back. She wanted to tell him she couldn't wait much longer to have him. She also wanted to savor every single moment of this. She reached for his boxers and moved them off of him. His size took her by surprise and she gripped him with her hand. He groaned and she moved her hand up and down his manhood. She reached the tip and rubbed her thumb over it. She thought he was going to come undone. And he did too. He kissed her hard on the mouth and pressed his manhood against her lower belly. He moved his mouth and tongue down her body, rolling her from side to side a little. He grinned when he saw the tiny hot pink heart inked on her left butt cheek. She did tell him she once worked at a tattoo parlor. He stopped at her core, and he teased her pleasure point until she damn near flew off of the bed. She moaned, she called his name, over and over, until she exploded onto his lips and inside of his mouth. He came up to kiss her hard and entered her as he did so. She was taken aback by the way he fit. The way he moved. His thrusts were slowly getting faster and he made her unexpectedly come again. Then moments later, he released himself inside of her. And they lingered as one for minutes on end afterward.

As they lay naked on his bed, limbs entangled and still touching and exploring each other's bodies to the point of wanting to do what they had just done to each other all over again, Audi spoke first.

"I think you should know something," she began, as he playfully pinched one of her nipples and she giggled.

"And what would that be?" he asked.

"You're hardly a boy," she stated, smiling.

"I'm relieved to know I convinced you," he said to her, stifling a laugh.

"Oh I'm more than convinced. I'm also madly in love with you, Delahunt. Every time you said it to me, wanting me to hear you and respond to you, I felt it and I wanted so badly to just tell you."

"I know," he said, because he really did know. "I could feel it."

"I love you, Wes Delahunt, and I need you in my life, in my bed. Forever."

"That can be arranged because I love you more."

And then he kissed her. *Mercy, did he ever kiss her.*

Epilogue

6 weeks later, Audi and Wes returned to the B&B. As soon as they drove up, Audi glanced over at the swingset. Wes saw her, and reached for her hand. He understood everything about her. Just when she thought she couldn't love him any more than she already had, she did.

They were holding hands when they walked inside of the B&B. The excitement on both Gran and Nurse Jo's faces warmed Audi's heart to no end. It was apparent how happy they were for her. For them. And for what she and Wes had found together amid a hurricane of pain and despair.

Audi was still contemplating how to tell Gran that she and Wes decided together to live in his country home in Utah. They would visit the B&B every weekend if she wanted to, Wes had assured her. At Gran's age it would be more difficult for her to travel, they both knew. They all had a lot to discuss right now. Gran had some news of her own to share. She was considering closing the B&B. She and Nurse Jo had spoken at length and agreed the amount of work there was exhausting for them, especially without someone as young as Audi to help.

Everything would work out, and fall into its place eventually. Gran believed that with all of her heart, especially when a young man and a baby showed up at the B&B a few days ago. They were there again now, as Gran had asked for them to return upon Audi's arrival back home.

Audi glanced behind Gran and Nurse Jo, standing in the foyer. She saw a young man with tattoos up and down his forearm. Audi never judged anyone. And besides, this man had kind eyes. She moved her body to the side a little so she could see past Gran who was blocking her view, and that's when Audi saw her. The young man was holding Janey. Audi looked at Gran and Nurse Jo. *They knew something.*

"Hello, ma'am," the young man spoke first. "I'm Jane's dad."

"You came to visit? You have no idea how much this means to me. Gran, you should have told me!" Audi felt ecstatic. She truly thought she would never see, or hold, that baby again.

"I came for more than a visit," the young man started to explain. "Her mom is gone. I don't have a good job. I have family, but they don't have much to offer. I can't possibly ever give my daughter all you gave to her in just a week. Most of all, you loved her and cared for her. She deserves that. If you still want her?"

Audi covered her mouth with her hand. *If she still wanted her?* She glanced at Wes. He was a permanent part of her life now. He had to be okay with that. All he did was simply nod his head and place his hand over his chest.

The One You're Waiting On

"I want her, oh my goodness, I want her! I don't know how to thank you for this," Audi told the young father, with tears pooling in her eyes and a wide smile that lit up her entire face.

"You can, by telling her I loved her so much, but I knew what was better for her. And that's you."

Audi's heart was so full right now, she feared it would burst. She thought of Berkley and all the blessings she was sending down to her from heaven. She was certain her little girl was whispering into God's ear. And then she thought of the gift she had been given in Utah. It was early yet, but she had known. She and Wes had already conceived a baby together. With both Janey and their baby on the way, life was going to be quite eventful with Delahunt for a very long time. And Audi was going to appreciate, savor, and take in every single blessed moment. She was ready to live again. What she was waiting on, to be happy and fulfilled again, was right in front of her.

ABOUT THE AUTHOR

I never planned for this story to take a tragic turn. It just did. And when it happened, I desperately wanted to find a way for Audi to pull through what is every mother's worst nightmare.

And if I could not find a way (as I kept writing), I was going to delete several chapters, start over, and completely change the story.

Mothers who have lost children must be some of the strongest women on this earth. Life has to go on, but I cannot imagine it continuing easily or without a constant pain and emptiness. What I hope becomes the focus of this story is how Audi eventually finds a reason to live again. She (like Gran told her to do) opened her heart to other blessings.

For all of you who are struggling with loss, may you find a way to go on, a means for comfort and contentment.

As always, thank you for reading!

Love,

Lori Bell

Made in the USA
Lexington, KY
22 April 2017